The First Year: A Marble Grant Novel

Ghost Diet & Other Marble Grant Stories

Ashes to Weddings & Other Marble Grant Stories

A Big Twisted Plot & Other Marble Grant Stories

PACKET JONES

The Big Tom: A Packet Jones Short Novel

Big Eyes: A Packet Jones Short Novel

THUNDER MOUNTAIN

Thunder Mountain

Monumental Summit

Avalanche Creek

The Edwards Mansion

Lake Roosevelt

Warm Springs

Melody Ridge

Grapevine Springs

The Idanha Hotel

The Taft Ranch

Tombstone Canyon

Dry Creek Crossing

Hot Springs Meadow

Green Valley

SEEDERS UNIVERSE

Dust and Kisses: A Seeders Universe Prequel Novel

Against Time

Sector Justice

Morning Song

The High Edge

Star Mist

Star Rain

Star Fall

Starburst

Rescue Two

COLD POKER GANG

Kill Game

Cold Call

Calling Dead

Bad Beat

Dead Hand

Freezeout

Ace High

Burn Card

Heads Up

Ring Game

Bottom Pair

THAT LOST RIDDLE & OTHER POKER BOY STORIES

DEAN WESLEY SMITH

WMG PUBLISHING

Contents

Introduction

The title story of this collection is about one of Lady Luck's daughters. I have written three stories about three of the daughters, but not the fourth one. Some day I will get around to it and more than likely then put all four stories in a book all their own..

The last story in the collection is about Lady Luck herself, sort of. It is the story where Poker Boy and Patty and his team really become special to Lady Luck and the rest of the gods and superheroes.

A lot of the stories in this volume are in the early years of Poker Boy, including the very first Poker Boy story "The Old Girlfriend of Doom."

And in some of these stories, Poker Boy has not moved to Las Vegas yet, but is still playing in a casino in the coast range mountains of Oregon and living in an old double-wide even though he is stunningly rich. He just likes it.

So I hope you enjoy these stories of the early days of Poker Boy. Amazing how he has grown over the decades and gotten more powerful.

Dean Wesley Smith
Las Vegas, Nevada

THAT LOST RIDDLE & OTHER POKER BOY STORIES

THAT LOST RIDDLE

THAT LOST RIDDLE

Out of thin air I heard Stan, the God of Poker say, "Knock, knock."

It wasn't a bad joke. It was how he asked to come into my private doublewide trailer up in the woods in Oregon. It seems that when Stan teleported, he couldn't just drop in outside and then use the door to actually knock on. But he was a God, and my boss, so I supposed he could do just about anything he wanted, even make bad "knock-knock" sounds in thin air in my living room. I was only Poker Boy, a lowly superhero. Not much I could say about it.

I pushed aside the cold fried chicken I had been eating while sitting on my old green couch and watching the evening news out of Portland. "Come on down."

Stan appeared beside my couch and glanced around, shaking his head. He always did that when he came here. He just didn't understand why someone with as much money as I had (and as many superpowers) would keep an old, 1970s-furnished doublewide trailer in the Oregon Coastal Mountains, even if it was within a half mile of a casino.

It was the green couch and chair and shag carpet that did it for most people, not counting the fake wood paneling on the wall. I figured if I waited long enough the styles would come around.

The last time Stan had come here he suggested I put a felt painting of dogs playing poker on the wall. I was considering it.

My girlfriend and sidekick, Patty Ledgerwood, aka Front Desk Girl, couldn't figure out why I liked this place either, now that she knew how much money I really did have. I discovered I had a vast amount when Patty made me go through it and lay it all out for her. I hadn't bothered to total it in a decade. I just kept adding to it.

Even though I could afford a couple dozen mansions, I liked this old place, even though Patty said it smelled of faint mold and pine trees. It reminded me of my early days as a poker player and superhero. The old furniture and funky smell sort of kept me grounded. I said that to Patty once and she just shook her head and muttered something about how the place kept me actually in the dirt.

Needless to say, we spent most nights in her wonderful and very large apartment in Las Vegas, furnished with the best and most modern furniture, thick carpet, and views of Las Vegas that were tough to beat.

I usually only came up here while she was working and I was waiting for a tournament to start. Instantly jumping from Las Vegas to the mountains of Oregon was one of the many advantages of being able to teleport.

Stan didn't say anything after his disgusted look at my place. He was wearing his standard tan sweater, tan slacks, and loafers. He looked so nondescript, he could blend in anywhere and no one would notice him. I had a hunch if he stood in my trailer long enough, his sweater and slacks would turn 1970s green.

I took one more bite of the cold chicken leg, then stood and headed for the coat hanger beside the front door to get my black leather coat and black fedora-like hat. They were my superhero uniform that helped make me Poker Boy.

Stan only came here to get me when something was going wrong somewhere. Never a good sign. So the coat and hat were going to be needed for something very soon.

"So where to?" I asked as I slipped on my coat.

"You look like you need a drink," he said.

"What?" He knew I didn't drink. Never had and I sure couldn't see myself starting now.

I was about to say something about going back to my chicken and news when Stan jumped us to position beside a large white-marble pillar with people walking by. There were slot machines and a nearby restaurant. I could feel the power from the casino around us flowing into me.

The air smelled of prime rib and faint cigarette smoke. It took me only a second before I realized we were on the second floor, the mezzanine level, of the Eldorado Hotel and Casino in downtown Reno, Nevada.

To my left along the interior mall-like area was the Silver Legacy Hotel and Casino and beyond that the Circus Circus Hotel and Casino.

This interior mall area stretched for a very long three blocks and must have a couple dozen restaurants, shops and gift stores along its wide corridor. It was a nice place considering Reno's weather in the winter, allowing people to move between the three casinos without ever going outside.

I had always liked this interior mall and the feel of it. Some people said it reminded them of a huge cruise ship, only without ocean views and people getting seasick.

I glanced around. No one had noticed our arrival so I figured Stan had jumped us into a blind camera area.

"Back with your girlfriend in a moment," Stan said and vanished, leaving me alone.

I had no idea what the problem was, or why we were in Reno, but if he was going for Patty when she was still at work, I knew it couldn't be good.

I stepped away from the stone pillar and let my poker senses take in everything around me. A few people upset at losing, and one couple went past not happy, headed for the Silver Legacy. I caught part of a conversation about how the guy was angry with his wife flirting with another man. He was telling her so in no uncertain terms. It wasn't hard to miss, even without extra poker senses.

But I could sense nothing that would cause Stan to jump us to Reno and into the Eldorado.

Across from me was a brewpub full of younger patrons laughing and drinking. I'm not sure exactly when I started thinking of adults around age thirty as younger, but I did. Since I have been told that as a superhero, I have basically stopped aging at thirty even though I am over forty, I have no idea how jaded I was going to get by the time I reached one hundred.

Or two-hundred-plus like Patty. She still hadn't told me her real age. She just shook her head and said it didn't matter every time I asked. She didn't look a day over thirty either, but knowing there might be a few hundred years in age difference sometimes actually bothered me.

I felt a hand on my shoulder and the calming sense of Patty's touch. That was one of her super powers and I loved it.

And her. More than I wanted to admit to myself at times. We just fit together in seemingly every sense.

I turned around to look into her beautiful brown and very worried eyes. She was still dressed in the uniform of the MGM Grand Hotel front desk. A black skirt, white blouse and MGM dark vest with their hotel emblem on the right side.

Her long brown hair was pulled back tight as she kept it while working.

"Any idea what's going on?"

I shook my head, keeping my poker senses on full. I didn't

quite have a "Spider-Sense" like Spider-Man did in the comics, but I had a pretty good ability to know when danger was approaching and right now I could feel nothing.

"Where is Stan?" I asked.

"He went to get Screamer," she said.

"This can't be good," I said.

She nodded.

A moment later Stan appeared next to the stone column in the dead camera area. Screamer was with him looking just as puzzled.

Screamer had the ability to touch someone and get into their mind and their thoughts. He didn't have a distinctive look, more like Stan with the ability to blend into just about anywhere. He usually wore old jeans and a sweatshirt with the UNLV logo on it and tonight was no exception.

Screamer had gotten his name from his ability to put images into other people's heads. He often worked for the police and could put images so bad and so real into a suspect's mind that he could make the most hardened criminal scream. What he did could never stand up in a court, but he had solved a lot of crimes over the years.

And he had helped this team save the world a few times as well.

"All right," Stan said. "Let's go."

He turned toward the short staircase leading down around an ornate fountain and into another section of the Eldorado Hotel and Casino mezzanine level.

"What are we doing here?" Screamer asked a moment before I could.

"Going for a drink," Stan said, his voice almost lost in the sounds of the multiple fountains.

Patty just shook her head and I followed them, keeping every sense I had on full alert. And that was a lot of senses, so many in fact I hadn't named them all. But the one right now I was trusting the most was my danger awareness sense.

And it was flat coming up blank.

We went past a gift shop, down another short flight of stairs, and toward what looked to be a combination bakery counter, restaurant on the right, and bar in the back on the left, tucked against the wall.

Suddenly Patty said, "Sherri."

Her uniform morphed into a black dress, her hair flowed into a perfect shape around her head, and black high heels replaced her tennis shoes she wore while working.

All in the space of one step.

I had no idea she could do that.

None at all.

And we'd been together now for a few years. If we survived whatever we were facing, we were going to need to have a talk about her powers.

"Oh, no," Screamer said as Stan headed toward the bar past the huge counter full of very tasty-looking pies and cakes and cinnamon rolls coated an inch deep in white frosting. The entire area smelled of fresh bread, making my stomach rumble and me wish I had taken a few more bites of that cold chicken.

"Come on, Stan, why?" Screamer asked.

Stan said nothing. Just kept walking.

Stan reached the bar and pulled up a barstool. Screamer sat on his left, Patty took the spot on his right, and I took the spot next to Patty.

I could still sense absolutely nothing wrong, but from Patty's sudden change and Screamer's comment, they were clearly sensing something I wasn't.

And that scared me more than I wanted to admit.

We sat there in silence with the sounds of the distant casino echoing faintly in the background. It must have only been a few seconds, but it felt like an eternity.

The bar was a normal wood bar, pretty wide, and even though it looked rustic, it was polished as smooth as glass. We were the only customers sitting at it. There were three empty stools to my right. It felt really, really strange to be sitting at a bar. I just never did this.

Bottles of varied booze lined the ornate back bar, blocking most of a mirror that made the area seem bigger. The top of the back bar was also a rustic ornate wood as were all the decorations on both sides of it.

This kind of bar could have been in any one of a thousand places. It actually seemed a little out of place with all the desserts in a huge counter ten paces behind us. It felt like it belonged more in an Old West saloon in a movie. A long ways from the smell of baking bread and ringing modern slot machines.

I was about to say something when a door into a back room swung open and a stunning woman emerged carrying a few bottles of vodka. She wore tan slacks, a white short-sleeve blouse, and an apron with the Eldorado Hotel logo on it. Her pitch-black hair was pulled back tight and I caught a glimpse of a dark tattoo on her shoulder and upper arm.

And she might have been one of the most beautiful women I had ever seen.

"Hey, Stan," she said, smiling in a way that could knock down just about anyone with its radiance.

Now my warning senses were going off and going off strong. If she was sitting across from me in a poker tournament, I would be very, very careful even being in a hand with her. She had power. More than likely she was a superhero or maybe a god.

But I caught no threat at all of danger from her. Just warnings about her power.

Stan nodded and didn't return the smile. "Sherri," was all he said.

She put down the bottles, wiped her hands on a white bar towel and slipped a bar napkin in front of Stan.

"Great seeing you," she said. "I suppose Mom sent you and your team here."

"She did," Stan said, again nodding.

"Well, I appreciate you coming," she said, smiling. "Thanks."

I wanted to shout out *"Mom?"* but then realized the only woman who could order Stan, the God of Poker around, was Laverne, Lady Luck herself. I now had a hunch suddenly who I was facing. I hadn't known going into a previous mission that Lady Luck had a daughter, so I suppose it shouldn't surprise me that she had two.

Or more for all I knew.

When this was over, I really needed to ask some very pointed questions about the family trees of some of my bosses.

Sherri put a bar napkin in front of Screamer, the smile turning a little sad on her face.

"I miss you," she said.

He only nodded just slightly, his gaze holding hers.

She missed him?

What in the world was going on? If this Sherri was Lady Luck's daughter, having both Stan and Screamer have strange reactions to her didn't seem like much of a good start to whatever we were facing here.

She shrugged and moved to a spot in front of Patty. She slid a napkin in front of her and smiled, the smile actually reaching her eyes. "Patty Ledgerwood I presume. I've heard so many good things about you and your work. You look stunning."

Patty smiled, blushed, and said nothing.

Sherri slid a napkin in front of me, her smile turning to something I couldn't read.

"So this is the famous Poker Boy I've been hearing so much about."

I kept my poker face and only nodded slightly.

She laughed. "You people sure aren't much for idle conversation, are you?"

"We're here," Stan said, his voice very controlled. "I don't understand why you are here, or what you need from us."

"I work here," she said, smiling. "I have now for about four years. Moved here from the Atlantis Casino. I worked there for ten years. Remember?"

She looked at Screamer and he just nodded.

She went on. "The management here keep offering to make me a bar manager, but I like keeping my hand in the drinks and talking with the customers."

Even though Stan had the best poker face that existed, I could tell he was surprised by that. If this was Lady Luck's daughter, I was surprised as well.

"And I didn't ask you to come here," Sherri said. "That was Mom's idea. She said you four might be able to help me with my lost riddle."

Stan said nothing, Screamer just shook his head, and Patty just smiled softly and stared at her.

Wow, was there a lot of history between these four. Clearly it had all happened long before I was born. And since Stan had been married to one of Lady Luck's daughters, more than likely he wasn't pleased to see this one either. So it looked like this was going to be up to me to figure out what she was talking about.

"So what's the riddle that your mom thought we could help you solve?" I asked. "And I assume I am talking with a daughter of Lady Luck. Correct?"

"Sherri," she said, giving me that beaming smile that I had no doubt melted some of the icing off a cinnamon role in the case behind me.

"The Queen of Clubs," Screamer said, his voice soft.

"Dear husband," Sherri said, a slight touch of hurt going to her eyes, even though she kept smiling. "You used to not like anyone calling me that name."

I was trying to deal with the fact that Screamer had been married to Lady Luck's second daughter at one point. Now all I had to do was figure out why Patty had a problem with her and I might have a clue what was happening.

"So the riddle?" I asked, pulling her attention back to me. "What's so important about it?"

"It's lost," Sherri said over her shoulder to me as she moved fluidly down the bar to pour some drinks for a waitress that had come up to the waitress station in front of a bar well.

Sherri seemed to move faster than anyone I had ever seen, yet the waitress never once looked up. After only a moment, which I guessed had something to do with her slipping slightly out of time to do the drinks, she came back toward us wiping her hands on a bar towel. "Can I get any of you a drink?"

My three teammates sat silently, so I said, "Sure. Bloody Mary mix with no vodka."

"Celery?" she asked as she moved to the well again.

"Nope," I said.

As she finished my virgin drink, I studied her. Not one sense of danger, nothing from her, and she wasn't blocking me in any way. In fact, I wasn't getting that much sense that she actually had many powers at all, even though I assumed she was a god. Could it be that Lady Luck's daughter was only a superhero like I was? That didn't seem possible.

As she put the drink on my bar napkin and again wiped off her hands, I asked her a simple question. "What's so important about finding or solving the riddle?"

"It will lead me to a second key holding the Four Faces of Janus."

"Oh," was all I said.

Stan just shook his head.

Screamer sort of snorted in disgust and Patty again didn't move.

We had already gone into Elysium, the capital of the ancient race of the Titans, to rescue Sherri's sister, Helen the Queen of Hearts, who had gone there to get one of the keys that held the Four Faces of Janus.

Supposedly, legend says that when the four keys are combined, they will open the time lock and allow the Titans to return to their rightful place in time and space. Or something like that. Mythology and facts were sometimes hard to tell apart for me these days. I really, really needed to ask more questions about all this.

One thing I did know, the Titans' major city existed in the same location as Las Vegas, only many, many eons in the future. So their coming back to this time would be a pretty large problem that I doubted anyone wanted to face.

"Are all your sisters looking for a key?" Stan asked.

"Sure," Sherri said. "It's sort of a hobby for all four of us. We're giving the keys to Mom for safekeeping when we find them. We have no intention of bringing them together, especially after seeing the wonderful city the Titans are living in."

"And you four have only found the one key, right?" I asked, trying not to be too stunned at Lady Luck having four daughters. I really, really, really needed to talk with someone about who had been married to whom and who was a child of whom.

"Just the key that you four helped my sister return with from Elysium," Sherri said, "although I feel that if I could find the lost riddle, I would be able to retrieve the second one."

Her bright smile had now vanished and she was clearly thinking about her problem. And I had zero idea what she was talking about when she said a "lost riddle" and my glowering team was sure no help at the moment.

"How can a riddle be lost?" I asked, slightly fearful I was walking into some trap.

Sherri just shrugged. "Lost in time, maybe. Never written down. Lots of ways a riddle can be lost."

"So it's just called "The Lost Riddle?" I asked.

She nodded.

Now all four of us were just looking at her as she headed back down the bar to the right to serve drinks to another waitress who had arrived at the station there.

"Someone want to tell me what's going on?" I asked.

"I think she's finally lost it," Screamer said, shaking his head sadly.

"She's fantastically beautiful," Patty said. "More than I even remember."

I stared at my girlfriend for a moment, realizing she hadn't been mad at Sherri, she had just been in some sort of fan-girl state with her.

"She's serious, all right," Stan said. "And she's as sharp as she ever was, trust me."

"So why do you hate her so much?" I asked Stan.

He laughed, softly, something I rarely heard him do. "I don't hate her. My wife, her sister, thought I fell in love with Sherri and caused all sorts of problems that led to me leaving Helen."

"You didn't?" I asked. "Fall in love with Sherri, that is?"

Again Stan just laughed. "I don't even really know her, to be honest. And Sherri's been married to Screamer here for a very long time."

"Over two hundred years," Screamer said.

"And she left you?" I asked.

"No, I left her," he said. "When I acquired this new power and could read all her thoughts every time I touched her. Staying together wasn't fair to either of us until we figured out how to deal with it all. We never got a divorce. It's been ten years now."

"So you are still married?" Patty asked, looking at Screamer, who nodded.

"Oh," was all I could say again. I had been working with this team now for some time and seen the inside of Screamer's mind more than I wanted to think about, and he had kept all this blocked from me. Clearly he had gotten pretty good at walling off parts of his own thoughts.

"She's so beautiful," Patty said, almost sighing. "We have to help her."

Now both Stan and I were shaking our heads at my girlfriend. Everything was screwy about this assignment and it was making me slightly annoyed. No one was in danger, I wasn't saving anyone, not even a dog, and I wasn't playing in a poker tournament. So far all I could see was a complete waste of a perfectly good evening.

Sherri again came back to a place in front of us. "Will you help me?"

"A couple more questions," I said. "So you need this riddle to find the Janus key?"

She shook her head. "I know where the key is at."

"So why do you need the lost riddle?" I asked, almost afraid of the answer.

"Stan," Sherri said, smiling at my boss, "If you wouldn't mind taking us all out of time for a moment, I'll answer Poker Boy's question."

He shrugged and an instant later the sounds of the casino stopped around us. And so did everyone and everything else.

I loved being able to step between an instant of time. One of my abilities was also to take myself and others out of the natural time flow. But Stan was a ton better at it and wouldn't have to strain to hold this for hours.

Sherri pointed to a place in the air behind her and an image like a three-dimensional movie appeared.

"That's new," Screamer said, looking puzzled.

"Learned it from you, actually," Sherri said, smiling at her husband. "It's a projection from my mind."

"I can't do that," Screamer said.

Sherri looked almost longingly at her husband. "We both have our new powers. I would love to talk later."

I was starting to get the clear understanding that she wasn't a god, but only a superhero like three of us at the bar. And she was learning new superpowers as she went along just as all superheroes did.

She turned back to the image she was projecting in the air as everyone in the casino remained frozen in their instant of time around us.

The image showed what looked like an old ghost town from a height of about a thousand feet in the air.

"Virginia City," Sherrie said. "South and slightly east of here."

The view came down and focused on some old buildings, then flew inside like a bird going through a wall. "Yellow Jacket Mine," she said. "Part of what most people think of as the Comstock Lode."

The traveling view of the image floating in the air went straight down, under some water and finally came into a flooded huge cave.

Sherri went on narrating the tour that was coming from her own mind. "The Yellow Jacket Mine broke into this huge cave and couldn't contain the flooding and had to retreat. No pump could ever clear it. It's over three thousand feet under Virginia City and the water temperature is over one hundred and fifty degrees."

At the bottom of the huge cave was a stone stand with a clear glass bubble covering it and protecting what looked like a very old key from the water.

"That's the second Janus key," Sherri said, her voice wispy.

"Why couldn't these stupid keys ever be hidden above ground?" I asked, shaking my head. My warning senses were going off big time just looking at that key so far down underground and underwater.

"So why the lost riddle?" Patty asked, the spell of Sherri's beauty clearly now broken by the little tour underground.

The image of the submerged cave vanished and Sherri just shrugged. "Not a clue what the riddle does," she said. "Or even what it is or why it's lost. I just know it's attached to this key in some fashion. And we don't dare touch the key until we understand what the riddle is all about."

I just shook my head. "This is a very strange hobby you and your sisters have."

Sherri laughed high and light. "Don't you think I know that? But after you guys helped my sister get the first one, Mom thinks it would be a good idea to get all four of them and get them really protected. So she's trying to help us."

I didn't want to say that having a key three thousand feet underground in one-hundred-and-sixty degree water wasn't already pretty protected, but what did I know? Lady Luck thought this was important for some reason. And she was Stan's boss and Stan was my boss, so by that reasoning I thought this important as well.

Stan let us slip back into the normal stream of time and the noise from the restaurant and distant casino slammed back into use like a tidal wave. And the wonderful smells from the restaurant came back as well, making my stomach rumble again.

"Okay," I said, trying to grab onto something that made sense in all this. "Tell me when I get this wrong."

Stan and Patty nodded and Sherri and Screamer just sort of looked at each other.

I ignored them and started trying to check off what I knew. "The four keys each have one side of the face of Janus on them. Right?"

Sherri and Stan both nodded.

"Apart they keep the doors locked, the Titans in the future, and the war between the Gods and the Titans stopped," Sherri said.

"Got that," I said. "And no one wants to start that war again."

"Exactly," Stan said.

"Does this Janus still exist?"

"No," Sherri and Stan said at the same time. They clearly

did not like that question and I made a note to ask what happened to him at a later date.

"So why would anyone associate a riddle with a key?" I asked. "And then lose all record of the riddle? I've only been around this superhero and god world for a short ten or so years and I've come to realize that all you folks have very long memories."

"Good question," Stan said. "But the battle between the Gods and the Titans was long before any of our times. Long before Atlantis."

I nodded to that. I still have never asked exactly how many years all this stretched back. Another question for another time in my history lesson.

I leaned back and just stared up at the back bar. No one else said a word and Sherri moved back down the bar to serve another waitress with a tray full of dirty glasses and a long order of fresh drinks.

I tried to ignore my rumbling stomach and my desire for a cinnamon roll and just think.

On the back bar were a number of bottles of Jack Daniels, all with different colors and added names on the labels.

There were other bottles of the same brand, but different types back there as well. I stared at that for a moment and then it suddenly hit me what we were dealing with.

Being able to put things that made no sense together to make sense was one of my super powers, it seemed, and if I was right, I had just done it again.

"Stan, could you call Laverne to come and help us?"

He nodded and a moment later, without him moving, Lady Luck appeared, taking the empty stool to my right.

In my fondest dreams as a poker player, it never would have occurred to me that I would be sitting at a bar with Lady Luck herself.

Sherri finished the orders and came down the bar as her mother appeared.

"You want your usual, Mom?" she asked, smiling. Clearly the two of them had a good relationship.

"Later, honey," Lady Luck said. "First I want to hear what Poker Boy has to say about all this."

For the first time in a long time I wished I actually drank. I had a hunch I could use one right now. I took a deep breath and turned toward one of the most powerful gods that existed and asked the question I needed to ask.

"Do the keys have names besides one, two, three, and four?"

Lady Luck looked at me for a moment, then laughed and said, "I don't know, but I know who to ask."

She vanished.

I decided I could breathe again. It felt good.

I took a sip out of my Virgin Bloody Mary as Patty touched my leg and sent a calming sense through me.

"You think the key might have a name?" Sherri asked, clearly puzzled.

Stan just smiled and Screamer sort of smiled. They had seen me ask these kind of questions before that got right to the heart of a problem.

"Just an idea," I said.

It seemed like forever, but then suddenly Lady Luck was again sitting at the bar beside me.

And she was laughing.

"The one you all retrieved from the Titan's city under Vegas was called *Mystery*. The two that have not been found yet are called *Enigma* and *Dilemma*."

Then Lady Luck smiled at Sherri. "The one you found, dear daughter, is called *Riddle*."

Sherri clapped her hands together and did a little dance as she laughed and smiled. "It's not protected!"

"I'll get it," Lady Luck said, smiling at the joy her daughter felt.

She vanished and then a moment later reappeared holding the key that had been under three thousand feet of Earth and very hot water. She wasn't wet at all.

She started to hand the key to her daughter who held her hands up. "I don't want to touch it. Just get it safe and sound."

"I will," Lady Luck said.

Then she turned to me. "Once again, Poker Boy, thank you. And to your team as well for taking the time to help with this."

It never got old having Lady Luck thank me for helping her.

Never.

Then Lady Luck looked down the bar at Screamer and

smiled. "Talk to your wife. If you two got back together, she'd make a great addition to this team."

"Mom!" Sherri said, but Lady Luck was already gone.

For the first time Stan really laughed. And hard. And that also was a rare thing as well for the God of Poker.

"Great seeing you again, Sherri," Stan said. "And listen to your mother. We could use you." Then he vanished.

Sherri actually blushed.

Patty smiled at Sherri and then at Screamer and touched my leg. "Come on, I'm dressed up and I think I need to do some dancing."

"Dancing?" I asked, looking at her. In all our time together she had never told me she liked to dance. Ever.

She winked at me and squeezed my leg just a little higher and I got the message. "Oh! *Dancing*."

A moment later we were in the living room of her apartment in Las Vegas, leaving Sherri and her husband alone in a crowded casino in Reno.

"Wasn't she beautiful?" Patty asked as she headed for her bedroom.

"Sherri?" I asked. "She was all right, but not as beautiful as you by a long ways."

"You sure know how to say the exact right things," Patty said.

She looked back over her shoulder at me and smiled a "dancing smile" as her dress vanished, leaving her totally naked and me totally speechless.

The Old Girlfriend
of Doom

Chapter One

Sometimes even superheroes can't save the day, or the girl, or the dog, and that fact is even sadder when the girl is one of the superhero's old girlfriends.

Honest, Poker Boy, and just about every superhero, once had a childhood, a life as a young adult, without powers. I only discovered my Poker Boy super abilities later in life, after I had lived a fairly regular life until the age of twenty-nine. Little did I know that some day I would put on the black leather jacket and the fedora-like hat and become Poker Boy, savior of blind women, lost husbands, and dogs.

It was Christmas Eve, a holiday for me just about like every other one. I was home, alone, in my double-wide mobile home that I had bought twenty years ago with the money from my winnings in a poker tournament. The green couch and chairs had come with it, and so far I had seen no reason to replace the perfectly good, but dog-ugly furniture. As a national-level poker player, I had more than enough money in a dozen accounts to buy a nice home, and nice furniture, but since I was in poker rooms and hotels more than I was here, what was the point?

Besides I spent most of my time with Patty Ledgerwood, aka Front Desk Girl in her apartment in Las Vegas. She was working tonight, pulling a double shift, so we had no plans until later in the week.

I was watching some lame Christmas program on television and eating a television dinner with fried chicken and the really good cherry desert. I had about two hours to get to the casino to sign up for the poker tournament, and I was enjoying the quiet, to be honest.

Then there was knock on my door.

As Poker Boy, I very seldom have the people who need help come to me, but there have been exceptions. And since I wasn't expecting any company, I figured right off this was one of those exceptions.

I opened the front door of my double-wide mobile home and saw my old girlfriend, Julie Down, standing there on the other side of the screen door. Of course, right at that moment I didn't know it was Julie. All I could see was that it was some woman about my age with a nice smile and an over-built chest.

"Hi," Julie said, smiling at me as I stood there, hand on the wooden door, staring at her though the screen.

Now I have a great memory for faces across poker tables. I

can tell you the moment a person sits down if I have played with them before, the style of their play, and their poker tells. I won't remember their names, but I know the important stuff and how to take their money.

With old girlfriends, from the life before I became the superhero Poker Boy, I am lucky to even remember going out with them, let alone things like their names, or if we slept together. I assume that any old girlfriend coming to find me years later is someone I must have slept with.

On top of my bad memory, Julie didn't look like the Julie of old. Granted, I'm forty-nine in human years, and Julie and I were an item back twenty-five years before, when she was only twenty. But that said, she just didn't look the same. Not even close.

Julie of old had long blonde hair that had touched the top of her butt. I remember I used to love laying in bed and watching that hair flow over her back as she walked naked around the bedroom. This Julie standing in front of me had tight, short graying hair, curled in a style that made her look older and very business-like.

Julie of old was rail thin, with no real breasts to speak of, and no body fat at all.

This Julie had filled out, as all of us have. She wasn't fat, but she wasn't that light and rail thin either. And she had had a boob job at some point. Or one hell of a growth spurt focused only on her chest. The white blouse she now wore under her open suede jacket made sure that everyone could see the growth spurts and the lace bra trying to hold back the progress.

"Hi," I said in return, at that point not yet knowing who the hell I was talking to. I wished at that moment that I had my black leather jacket and hat on, and was closer to a casino. Then I could use my super powers to help me figure out exactly what this woman wanted to sell me.

Or wanted me to do.

"You don't remember me, do you?" she said.

Okay, I have to admit that those words are the worst words any guy can ever hear from some strange woman standing at his door. I didn't have a clue who she was, yet she remembered me well enough to track me down.

A guy is never allowed to forget a woman.

Ever.

I glanced at her boobs, and since they were new since the last time I saw this woman, they didn't help. And her face rang a sort of bell when I looked right at her, and into her eyes, but not much of a bell. Actually, sort of a faint ding, like an oven timer going off in another room.

If I hadn't been a superhero, who didn't lie unless it was to save a life, or rescue a dog, I would have just laughed and said, "Sure I do, come on in." And then tried to figure out who she was through the conversation.

But she had asked me a direct question, and being a superhero, I couldn't lie. So instead I said, "I can't really see you very well in this light. Come on in."

I honestly couldn't really see her that well in the porch

light and through the screen door, so I didn't lie. I just bought a little needed time.

As I swung open the screen door to let her come inside, she let me off the hook.

"It's me, Julie."

For a moment, as she stepped past me, leading into the room with those new growth spurts on her chest, I couldn't remember any Julie's in my life either. Especially Julie with a chest the size of the Rockies.

"Julie Down," she said, ending all torture.

"Oh, my god, Julie," I said, "what a great surprise."

Actually I sounded happy mostly because she had let me out of the trap, and not because I was actually glad to see her. The last time we had spoken, she had called me a lazy bum, said I would amount to nothing, and that I should get a life. Or at least a reason for living and breathing.

Actually, at the point she left me, I was a lazy bum, and I really did need a life, but I wouldn't find that life until a number of years later when I became Poker Boy.

In all, I think we dated seven months, or more accurately, had sex for seven months. I don't remember much else in the relationship with her.

After I gave her the required hug, with her growth spurts holding us apart, she stepped back and studied me, then my abode, like a meat inspector looking over a side of beef.

"You look like you're doing well for yourself," she said.

Even without my super powers I knew that was a lie. I was living in an old mobile home, with old, ugly furniture and a half-eaten t.v. dinner on the coffee table. I looked like, on the surface, the same guy she had gotten mad at twenty-five years before. If I had not had my Poker Boy identity, and a lot of money in different banks from all my poker winnings, I would have been ashamed that an old girlfriend saw me living like this. But superhero status, and large bank accounts tend to make a guy not care, and I didn't really care what she thought.

"Actually," I said, "I'm doing very well. Can I get you something to drink? Diet Coke and water are the options."

She laughed, a high, soft sound I remembered from our past. Her laugh had been one of the things that had attracted me to her back then. That, and sex.

Now I just wanted to know what she wanted. And the only way I was going to be able to do that with my super powers was get my coat and hat on, and get back into a casino.

My super powers don't work a great distance from a casino. They are powered by the energy of a casino, like a flashlight is powered by a battery. My black leather coat and hat seemed to focus the energy from the casino and make me into Poker Boy.

"Wait," I said, "I have another idea. Let me buy you dinner and a drink at the casino." I pointed to my partially-eaten t.v. dinner. "That just isn't doing it for me."

"That sounds great," she said.

No doubt she was clearly relieved to get out of the old mobile home.

CHAPTER TWO

Fifteen minutes of very, very small talk later, we were seated in the fine dining restaurant at the casino. I had my leather coat and hat on, and was in full Poker Boy power mode.

I knew with a quick scan with my Ultra-Intuition Power that she needed help. Poker Boy's help, actually, which was interesting that she had found me.

My Ultra-Intuition Power is my most used power. With a focused glance, I can tell what a person needs, what they might say next, or even their next action. The information comes to me by "little voice messenger" and I have learned to listen.

I could list all my super powers right now, but that would be a dull monologue, not worth the time since there are so many. Some of the powers I haven't even named.

"Thank you," she said to me after we were settled at a table and the waiter was off getting our drink orders.

"For what?" I asked.

"For being so welcoming, especially on Christmas Eve."

"Poker players are never much for Christmas," I said, shrugging. "The ones with the families miss days and sometimes weeks of play. The rest of us just continue on and mostly don't notice."

"You have no family?" she asked. "And you play poker for a living?" She sounded actually impressed about the second part.

"Right on both counts," I said. "How about you?"

She sighed, and then for the next twenty minutes, through drinks, appetizers, and into the main course, she told me about her family, her parents being sick, her brother being stupid, her last two husbands being abusive.

I wanted to ask her when the growth spurt on her chest had happened, but refrained. Some things you just don't ask a woman, I have learned, and that's one of them.

Suddenly, she stopped talking, afraid to tell me about something. She had been fairly graphic about her past husbands, what they had done to her. Some of it I couldn't believe she would just tell a stranger like me. Granted, we had a past, but after not seeing this woman for over twenty-five years, I was still a stranger.

She studied her salmon, forked it a few times, studied it some more, forked it again, all the time trying to say something. Whatever was now stopping her must be really something. It was, more than likely, the reason she had looked me up.

I used my Ultra-Intuition Power on her again, but could only see blackness.

Deep, deep blackness.

Not good, not good at all.

I needed another super power to help her out, get her to tell me her problem. I focused across the table at her, learning forward, clicking my mind into a friendly, giving mode. A moment later I felt the super power click on.

Empathy Super Power to the rescue.

I could make her feel better, I could make her trust me. My Empathy Super Power sort of radiated good feelings to another person, so it really wasn't empathy, by the standard dictionary definition, but Empathy Super Power was the only thing I could think to call it. I had tried Feel Better Super Power, but that had seemed silly. And so did Trust Me Super Power. So until I could come up with a better name, it was called my Empathy Super Power.

She looked up at me, her gaze holding mine. "I just feel like I can talk to you, and that you'll understand."

Empathy Super Power working just fine.

"I will," I said, easing my hand across the table between the water glasses and salt shaker to touch her hand.

Touch always made my Empathy Super Power even stronger.

"What's bothering you?" I asked.

She looked embarrassed for a moment, then took a deep breath and blurted out her problem.

"Aliens are trying to steal my breasts."

Chapter Three

I knew there were no such things as aliens, at least at the moment on the planet. There had been in the past, and I am sure there would be again. They visited all the time. But right none of them were around that I knew of.

But there were many, many other things that normal people confused with aliens. And there was an entire dark world that existed along with the light world we all lived in. It was against creatures from that dark world that I, and other superheroes, fought so often.

"Aliens?" I asked, keeping my touch on her arm and my super Empathy power turned on. "What do these aliens look like? Have you seen them?"

She nodded. "Gray, short, with long fingers and little round-shaped mouths."

"Big heads?" I asked.

"Yeah," she said, staring into my eyes. "Big for their bodies."

I could feel my stomach twist. She was even more trouble than I had thought.

"And they want your breasts?"

She nodded.

I sat back, pulling my hand away and shutting off the super power. "You're not dealing with aliens. Those are Silicon Suckers."

"Silicon Suckers?" she asked. "How do you know that?"

"I've had to deal with them a couple of times over the years," I said. "They're not a nice bunch, and you clearly have something they want, or they wouldn't be showing themselves to you."

I knew exactly what they wanted, but I was going to have to work into telling her what it was.

Silicon Suckers are a race of intelligent creatures that have existed on Earth far, far longer than human beings. They live in the deserts, burrow deep under the sand, and have the ability to change their appearance and blend with about anything. In this country Phoenix, New Mexico, and Las Vegas areas have the most trouble with them.

"Silicon Suckers?" she said. "My breasts are silicon implants." She was clearly starting to understand what the little guys were after.

I almost said, "Really, I hadn't noticed." But I stopped myself before that gaff and instead just nodded. Then I moved to the next question.

"Where have you been living?"

"Vegas," she said. "I've been working as a blackjack dealer at Circus Circus for the last six years, since I left Bastard Husband #2."

"Good for you," I said, actually impressed. I knew how hard, and how special it was to become a dealer on the strip. "When did you have the implants put in?"

"Twenty years ago," she said. "I did it between Bastard Husband #1 and Bastard Husband #2. But I upgraded them six months ago, and that's when the gray aliens started showing up."

"Oh, oh," I said. "Dr. Doubleday did the upgrade. Right?"

She looked at me as if I had lost my mind, then nodded. "How did you know that?"

Actually, I wasn't reading her mind or using any other super power. I had dealt with Silicon Suckers for a friend of a friend in Vegas five months before, on an adventure that also rescued three dogs. On that trip, I had discovered that Dr. Doubleday had been using a very special silicon mix taken from pure natural sand and then refined down into a very special silicon gel.

The problem was the sand he had been using was from a sacred Silicon Suckers burial site. Julie, my old girlfriend sitting across the table from me, had a real problem. She had dead Silicon Suckers for breasts.

CHAPTER FOUR

"I know because one of the things I do is help people as I travel around the country playing poker," I said.

"I know," she said. "I've heard about you. Some people call you Poker Boy."

Since she clearly looked as if she didn't believe what she had just said, I let it pass and went on. "I helped a previous client of Dr. Doubleday. I assume you tried to go back to him after the Silicon Suckers started showing up and playing with your breasts. And I bet you found him missing."

Now Julie was looking at me as if I was an alien.

I knew for a fact that Dr. Doubleday had given his life for trying to improve his craft and find the most perfect silicon implants. After what he had done to the Silicon Suckers sacred resting place, many of us in the superhero world thought he got off light by only being killed. His body will

49

never be found. More than likely parts of Dr. Doubleday are tinting car windows everywhere.

"How did you know he wasn't there?" she asked.

"Doubleday is dead," I said. "Killed by the Silicon Suckers."

She sat there in silence, first staring at me, then down at her salmon. Finally she said, "Let's assume that I believe what you're saying."

"No weirder than thinking aliens are trying to steal your breasts."

She shrugged. "True. So what do I do?"

I put another bite of steak in my mouth, savored the flavor for a moment. There was only one answer to her question.

"If you're going to want to live, you have to give them your implants back."

"I'm not going to do that!" she said, her hands going to the monsters on her chest as if to protect the big girls.

I kept eating, staying calm. "You have no choice. If you don't have the money, I can pay for an exchange operation for the silicon implants you have now. All they want is those implants. They don't want you to be flat chested."

There was no chance at that point that the rest of her salmon was going to be eaten. She scooted the plate away and stared at me.

"I was *not* flat chested before I had the implants," she said. "You know, you're totally nuts."

I wanted to remind her that she had come to me for help. That she thought aliens were trying to take her boobs, but I didn't. Instead I just gave her the rest of the information, calmly and slowly, keeping my voice level.

"The creatures you are having trouble with are not aliens, but they are after the special silicon Dr. Doubleday used in those implants. If you have the implants removed, I'll be glad to help you give them to the Silicon Suckers in a special exchange ceremony. You give them back what they want and you'll always be an honored guest in their sand castles."

She stared at me like she was seeing me for the first time.

"Sand castles?"

"That's what they call their homes. I've been in a few of them outside of Tucson and Las Vegas. Big, but very dusty and dry."

She stared at me again, then shook her head slowly from side to side.

"I knew better than to come to you," she said. "Even with Suzy's recommendation, I knew better."

She stood and thrust her chest out so far I was afraid she was going to go head-first into my steak. Somehow, she managed to remain standing, although she cast a very dark shadow over the table as her breasts pulled an eclipse on the overhead light.

"These are mine and I paid good money for them," she said, loudly, indicating what did not need to be indicated. "And I'm not letting any little gray alien suckers take them."

The guy at a table against the wall choked, then coughed, clearly trying not to laugh.

"Your choice," I said. "But I'm doing all right with money

and I would be glad to pay for replacements. Remember that. No strings attached. You can even make them bigger if you want."

"I'll give it some thought," she said.

"Don't take too long to decide," I said, staring up at her over the monster mountain range between us. "Silicon Suckers are not creatures to be played with. The only way they know how to get into a human body is through the anus, and trust me, taking those silicon implants out that way will not be fun. And more than likely fatal."

She sputtered, started to say something more, sputtered again.

I didn't blame her.

Finally she managed to get those sacred and very dead Silicon Suckers on her chest turned toward the door. Then, with one last withering glance at me, she stormed out.

The guy against the wall was laughing so hard I thought he would go face down in his soup.

For me, it really wasn't a laughing matter. She was in mortal danger.

I wanted to run after her and stop her, but I knew, for a fact, there was nothing I could do at this point. I certainly wasn't going to force her to have an operation. A woman's choice of what to do, or not do, with her body was not something a man, or a superhero, should get involved with. She was going to have to make that choice for herself.

For some reason that I didn't completely understand, Julie's entire self-image must have been tied up in what the

Silicon Suckers wanted back. And replacements might not be enough to matter to her.

I wished I understood Julie's side. I did understand the Sucker's side.

The guy against the wall finally coughed a few times, shook his head, and went back to eating. I stared at my steak for a moment, thinking over anything I might still do to help her. Without butting in on her rights to do with her own body as she saw fit, there wasn't much.

She had come to me for help, then refused it. As those of us in the Superhero business know, there are times you just can't help.

CHAPTER FIVE

I finished my steak, and just barely made it into the poker room in time for the seven o'clock tournament.

I won the thing and put the money in a jar on my kitchen counter, saved for Julie's operation. But I had a hunch she would never call me, because after the tournament, on the way home from the casino, I found a German Shepherd in the ditch beside the road. It had been hit by a car, but was still alive.

I rushed it to the local vet, but the dog died on Christmas morning.

On good adventures, I save people and dogs. I couldn't save the dog, so I had a hunch I hadn't saved the person either in this one.

But that didn't stop me from trying some more.

I tracked down Julie and called her the day after

Christmas with the hopes of trying to convince her to change out the breast implants. She heard my voice and hung up.

I called a few friends I knew in Vegas who could be trusted to go talk to her. Both of them said she got rude and angry at them the moment they brought up the subject, or my name.

Julie had made her decision, and by all the gambling gods, she was sticking with it.

Somehow, I had to convince her to change that decision.

I had to keep trying.

That's what superheroes did, usually against all odds and at some cost and danger to their own lives. And trying to convince any woman to change her mind always had danger involved.

So throwing all caution to the wind, I jumped on a plane and headed for Vegas. Besides, I wanted to spend some time with Patty and get her opinion on all this.

Julie wouldn't see me, and had me removed from the Circus Circus when I went up to her blackjack table and sat down. Even my Empathy Super Power couldn't cut through the anger, although it made the guard very nice and apologetic for escorting me to the door.

Since the direct approach hadn't worked, I headed out into the desert, to where I knew the Silicon Suckers had a pretty good-sized village. It was impossible to see unless you knew exactly what you were looking for, and I did. The entrance to this one was hidden right under a billboard beside the highway.

The entrance lead to a huge underground cavern cut out of the sand and rock and filled with castle-like buildings. I was welcomed into their castles, as I knew I would be, since I had helped them recover one of Dr. Doubleday's mistakes.

The main leader of this band clicked at me in Silicon Sucker language, and I used what I called my Understand Most Anything Super Power to talk with him, asking him for more time to convince Julie to get their sacred dead off her chest.

He clicked that he would give me two full moons, or something that meant two months.

I thanked him, backed from his castle in a show of respect, and went back to Vegas.

Patty told me what I had feared, that there was nothing I could do unless Julie decided for herself.

I left the message on Julie's answering machine that I had the money for the exchange, had contacted the best doctor in Vegas to do the job, and had prepaid for it. All she had to do was show up. I left the time and date and address of the doctor, the most famous and expensive in Vegas, hoping that might convince her to change her mind.

Nothing. She missed the appointment.

So I pulled some strings in the Casino Gods area of the superhero world, and got the Blackjack God named Danny to talk to her pit boss at work.

That didn't work.

I talked to her friends, even called her mother, then I set up another appointment for her with the great doctor.

Again she missed it.

So one last time, with Danny, the god of Blackjack keeping the pit boss busy at another table, I went in to talk to her.

She was shuffling and didn't see me coming.

When I slid the doctor's business card with a third appointment written on it across the table toward her, she glanced up, the anger in her eyes almost knocking me back a step.

"Why are you insisting in meddling in my life?" she demanded, ignoring the stares from the older couple sitting at the table.

"Because you are in real danger," I said, using every convincing power I could use in my super power collection. With this much energy turned on at a poker table, I could have convinced a world-class player I had a pair of deuces instead of aces.

Julie, on the other hand, was a little tougher. She just glared at me, so I went on.

"I have enough money to help. You won't ever see me again, but please, just do this. It's paid for."

She stared at me as I radiated super levels of good will and empathy and convincing. My superhero powers were on full tilt right at that moment, and for a second I thought she was faltering a little.

"I'm being honest with you," I said. "Your life is in danger. Please just do it, either with this appointment or on your own. It's your life, I know, and your body, but I care about your life."

Then I turned and walked away.

There was nothing else I could do.

I spent the night with Patty trying to sleep, then got back on the plane and went home.

I finally heard three months later that they had found her body face down in the desert, as flat-chested as the day she had come into the world.

I think back and wonder at times what more I might have done to convince her I knew what I was talking about. More than likely nothing. She needed to believe I was still the loser she left for abusive husband hell all those years before.

She needed to believe that those special breasts made her a better person. For her, a certain self-image was more important than life itself.

For me, Poker Boy, I have my hat, my leather coat, and my super powers. What more could I want out of life?

Nothing, except maybe winning every time. But even the best superheroes have to lose once-in-a-while. I learned that lesson on the poker tables, and with Julie.

Still, you have to feel bad for a person like Julie, caught in a self-image nightmare.

And besides, pulling those sacred suckers out of her ass just had to have hurt.

SIGHED THE SNAKE

Chapter One

"Poker Boy, the aliens are back."

Stan, the God of Poker, said those exact words to me as I sat in his office next to my sidekick and girlfriend, Patty, aka Front Desk Girl.

His office, glass-walled and floating invisible somewhere high above the Las Vegas strip, had felt cool and comfortable when we had entered from a hidden door at the MGM Grand Casino. The view just took your breath away as Las Vegas stretched out below, surrounded by desert and then mountains in the distance. The walls were invisible, so it felt as if Stan had put office furniture on a floating carpet. Only pictures of great poker players on the walls lined out where the room started and the air outside ended.

As we got seated, a United Airlines jet passed silently to our west, just below us, headed for the airport. I could only imagine what the passengers I could see through the window on that jet would have thought if suddenly Stan's office had become visible out their windows, with Patty and I sitting in front of his desk.

Sometimes Stan kept his office dark and dingy, like a back room at an old, downtown casino, straight out of the mob days. That was when he was in a bad mood or things were threatening. When he let it float above the city, as it was now, you knew Stan was feeling pretty darned good about life with the Gambling Gods.

But his casual statement about the aliens returning rocked me, and I studied his smiling face. Even with my black leather superhero jacket and Fedora-like superhero hat on, I didn't have the power to get a read on Stan. No one could get a read on the God of Poker, which was why he had the job. So I reverted to the most logical way to get an answer. I asked him.

"This makes you happy, the aliens being back?"

Patty had sat forward in her seat at the comment from Stan, her long brown hair flowing over her white blouse and dress slacks, her new uniform for work. She had just recently taken a job as customer relations at the MGM Grand Casino and Hotel, and we had been having lunch in the nifty little Greek place just off the downstairs promenade when Stan called us.

When I'm in Vegas, Patty and I not only work cases together, we are an item. Actually, she's my only item whether I'm in Vegas or not, but I haven't figured out a way to tell her that just yet. As Poker Boy, I'm not known for being a ladies man, or for having just one woman in my life either. I wasn't sure how she would react, but knowing Patty, she probably already knew. She seemed to sense things about me before I did. I figured it was one of her many superpowers. Thank heavens she didn't play poker.

"Actually," Stan said, "not so much happy as satisfied. I won the pool."

"The pool?" Patty asked, glancing at me with those wonderful brown eyes of hers before looking back at Stan.

"We had a pool as to when they would return," Stan said, his smile getting bigger. "I got it to within a month. We started the pool the day after they left."

"They've been gone since the late 1950s," I said. "I'm impressed."

Stan smiled even larger. "Thanks."

"So, why are we here?" Patty asked, shaking her head and sitting back. She worked the hotel side of the gambling industry. And even though she was a superhero working under Laverne, Lady Luck herself, Patty sometimes just didn't understand the nature of a gamblers' need to bet on things. The Gambling Gods had bets running all the time for one thing or another. It was what they did. The alien pool was no surprise to me.

"We need you two to make contact with their representative, find out what they are planning, that sort of thing. Right now he's sitting in a 2-4 no-limit game at the MGM Grand."

"Not over at the Bellagio, huh? I wonder why." I would have figured the aliens could afford the higher stakes.

"Not a clue," Stan said.

Now it was making sense to me. I hadn't been a superhero long enough to have met the aliens the last time they visited the planet, but from what I understood, they loved to gamble, which was why the Gambling Gods ended up being their major contact with the planet Earth. The world governments at the time had hated that, but in the end, had to live with it. I doubted anyone in the current world governments had even been briefed that aliens actually existed, let alone the Gambling Gods. The Gods, and the superheroes like Patty and me, tended to stay under the radar as much as we could.

"Is the alien any good at poker?" I asked, smiling at Stan.

Stan laughed. "Not a clue. He's new. Go find out."

The wonderful view from Stan's office faded, and Patty and I moved from sitting in front of Stan's desk to walking down the hallway toward the MGM Grand's poker room. Always took a second for the mind to adjust when Stan did that.

CHAPTER TWO

The poker room at the MGM Grand had been remodeled a few years back, and now was in the shape of an hourglass. It usually had a good ten games going at any one time, and ran daily tournaments that were pretty popular around town. They catered mostly to tourists, with a few local pros working the room. The big money and high-stakes games had moved over to the Bellagio a number of years back, but the MGM still had a loyal following and they spread a good game and ran a tight room.

"So, what do we do now?" Patty asked, clearly worried about meeting a real-life alien.

"Stop at the counter and stay close until I figure out what the guy wants. I'm going to take us in as much under cover as I can manage."

I had no idea why I was taking those precautions. It just

felt right, and as a superhero and a poker player, I had learned a long time ago to trust that feeling.

Patty reached over and squeezed my hand, then let go, which was a good thing. I always found it hard to concentrate when Patty was touching any part of me. Some parts more than others.

As we neared the room, I brought up my Don't-Pay-Attention-To-Me superpower and covered both of us. Someday I was going to have to give that superpower a better name, but describing the effect it had seemed as good as any name for the moment.

I got a rack of five-dollar chips from the front counter and moved toward the 2-4 no-limit table against one drab-colored wall. Four men and two women sat around the table. The two women were clearly together, clearly from some Midwestern state, and pretending to be in over their heads. They didn't even notice me.

The guy in the number four chair was a local pro named Dan, and he managed to see through my cloak and nod as I sat down. Dan stood no more than five feet tall, and usually wore a dress shirt and tan jacket that made him look more like an accountant taking a break from the office than a professional poker player. But I knew he was as sharp and mean as they came and made good money every day at this table. I had no intention of tangling with him.

The other two men were tourists, both with drinks in front of them, and both more interested in the women than in playing poker. That left the guy wearing a snakeskin cowboy hat, sunglasses, and a western shirt, sitting in the seat to the right of the dealer. The weirdest thing about the guy was his tiny nose and almost complete lack of chin. It was as if his face just sort of blended down into his neck and into his black shirt collar.

I sat down in the chair directly across the table from him and slipped the five hundred in chips out of my rack, stacking them neatly as he watched.

He lowered his sunglasses just enough to show me his dark, black eyes, then grinned without showing any teeth. "Poker Boy, I presume."

Dan jerked at the mention of my name, then just stared at me. Clearly, my reputation had gotten ahead of me. I ignored Dan and focused on the alien.

I got nothing, no read, no sense of any emotion at all.

I dug deep and put my best superhero Poker Boy poker-read on him, getting almost nothing but a strange, dark feel. That was getting me nowhere.

"I don't think I have had the pleasure," I said in return.

"Just call me Snake," the alien said, his voice as close to a hiss as I could imagine a human voice sounding.

I hated snakes. I didn't mention that to him. More than likely, he knew. Instead, I just nodded.

I folded the first two cards the dealer fired my way without looking, then watched as Snake glanced at his and folded as well. He had very thin hair sticking out from under his hat that looked combed back over dark scalp, and he also clearly had a dandruff problem, since flakes kept falling on his black shirt.

"It's been a long time," I said, aiming at him as much of my Make-Them-Relax superpower as I dared use. "At least fifty years."

"Nah, that wasn't my people," Snake said, again grinning under his sunglasses without really opening his mouth. His leather-like skin sort of moved in waves up his neck to his mouth and then back down and I thought for a moment I heard a faint rustling sound. "We haven't been here for a good ten centuries at least."

Oh, crap! Stan wasn't going to be happy with that information. More than likely it meant he hadn't won the pool after all. And he hadn't told me that there was more than one alien race out there.

I felt my stomach tighten into a tiny fist. I hoped like hell Stan and Lady Luck were listening in on this. And I hoped like hell I had managed to keep my best poker face on when Snake told me he was with a different alien race than we were expecting.

"So, what brings you to our little corner of the poker universe?" I asked, forcing myself to stay as calm as possible.

"Why does anyone come to Las Vegas?" Snake asked, glancing at the two women who were ignoring our conversation and flirting with the two men. One of the women had just pulled the last pot and both were laughing about their luck. I had a hunch they were better than just lucky and this flatlander hick routine was just a ruse to take money. And the two guys were going to be more than happy to give it to them.

Dan, the pro, was just shaking his head at their antics and mostly watching me and Snake. I would wager he wasn't real pleased at how his favorite table had shaped up today.

"So," I said, keeping my attention focused on the alien, "you came across vast distances in space to vacation, gamble, drink, and have sex?"

He nodded, glancing at the two cards the dealer had just given him. "That pretty much describes it."

He put a chip on his cards and again sort-of smiled at me, the rustling of his dry skin clearly loud enough to hear this time. It sent shivers down my back. Did I mention that I really, *really* hated snakes? Especially snakes with a bad dandruff problem.

He raised a smooth hundred and Dan folded at once.

"But mostly," Snake said, again pulling down his sunglasses just enough for me to see the pitch black eyes behind them, "I'm here to see if I can beat the best poker player in the game. You up for a little heads-up action, Poker Boy?"

Now, I had to admit that having the alien call me the best player in the game stroked my ego just a little. I knew I was good, but I didn't think of myself as the best by a long ways.

"What did you have in mind?" I asked as I glanced at my cards and flipped the low pair of fours back at the dealer. Any two cards that would cause that kind of raise from Snake had a small pair beat from the start.

"We each start with a million in chips," Snake said. "When one of us has them all, he wins. Blinds level at five hundred, one thousand."

Every sense in my body, and a couple of my superpowers as well, were screaming there was more to this than a simple game for a million bucks.

"So, what would you do with my million, assuming you won it?" Actually, it would be the Gambling God's money, not mine. I was fairly rich, but not rich enough to risk a million against some alien.

Snake smiled again without opening his mouth. Again his skin made that dry rustling sound and I tried not to show the shiver that was running up my back. This guy could really be helped by a little lotion.

The dealer flipped me a pair of tens this time around, and I folded them like they were a seven-deuce off. No point in actually playing at this point in the conversation. One of the women giggled and raised and both of the suckers staring at her chest called. Dan and Snake both folded.

Snake reached down under the table and pulled up a golden apple, placing it on the rail in front of him. "I assume you don't remember this."

I stared at the apple for a moment. The thing shone in the casino lights, begging for someone to take a bite out of it. My stomach clamped up so tight, I could hardly breathe. I was talking with a member of the alien race that had caused the legend of Adam and Eve. It sure had been a while since they had been here.

A very, very long time, actually.

"Plucked right from the Tree of Knowledge, I bet," I said, keeping my calm exterior as poker-faced as I could, pretending to not really care.

Snake's thin, eyebrows raised above the top edge of his sunglasses. I had surprised him, and for the first time, my poker sense told me this alien had a weakness.

"I am impressed," Snake said. "I was led to understand that your race in general had no long-term memory, that you destroyed your past, or worshipped it for monetary gain."

"For the most part you're right," I said. "But you still haven't told me what the real bet is."

Snake tapped the apple with a long finger. "Contained in the apple is the design and basics for a good dozen major inventions that would forward your race into the stars." He touched the thing again. "Anti-gravity, time control, teleportation. It's all in here."

I didn't mention to him that the Gambling Gods already had all of those things and humanity would discover them in their own sweet time. I wanted to see exactly what he was after in return.

"Nice," I said. "Worth a million I would say."

Snake shook his head, the rustling so loud this time that even one of the guys staring at the women's chest looked around.

"Your money means nothing to me," Snake said.

"I assumed as much," I said, glancing over at where Patty stood near the main desk. Her eyes were wide and now Stan and Laverne were standing beside her. Clearly they were listening.

I gave Snake the old poker stare. "So what do you want in return if you win?"

"Political sanctuary," Snake said. "And twenty of your acres of land with a privacy dome over it so I can build my own climate-controlled garden to live in."

"And if I win?" I asked.

"You get the information in the apple and I will leave the planet and never return."

I glanced at the poker front desk where Patty now stood alone. Clearly Stan and Lady Luck had heard and were off doing what they needed to do.

"Give me fifteen minutes to talk to my boss, and I'll see what I can do," I said, pushing my chair back and standing.

Snake put the apple away and nodded, glancing down at his new cards. "I'll be right here."

I motioned for the dealer to watch my chips and deal me out, pushed my current cards back at the dealer without looking at them, and headed toward Patty.

Chapter Three

We were ten paces down the hall away from the poker room when we suddenly found ourselves in Lady Luck's big office. Stan was pacing in front of Laverne's desk, and she was tapping her fingers, staring at a blank screen on her wall beside her desk.

After a moment an alien that looked exactly like the guy sitting in the poker room came on the screen. Only this guy wasn't hiding his snake-like body with four arms and two legs. He was also golden colored, with streaks of red and blue and bright orange along two sides. I had no idea how large he was compared to the guy downstairs, but he seemed much, much larger on the screen.

Who knew that alien life in the universe would develop from snakes as well as monkeys?

"Laverne," the snake said in perfect British English. "It is always a great pleasure."

"The pleasure is all mine, Commander," Laverne said, bowing slightly.

I just stared, more than likely my mouth open. Not often you see Lady Luck herself bowing to anyone.

"I was expecting your call," Commander said. "I assume you have encountered the Lacit fugitive."

"He is sitting in one of our poker rooms as we speak," Laverne said. "He has challenged Poker Boy to a wager: an apple's-worth of knowledge against political sanctuary in a heads-up game of no-limit poker."

Commander shook his head. "They do love that old apple trick. Their entire race seems to never tire of it. They cause more damage to young cultures than any other race."

"I'll take your word for that," Lady Luck said.

Commander frowned and glanced around at something off screen before going on. "We are not scheduled to arrive for another seventeen of your hours. You would do us a great favor by stalling him without giving him political sanctuary. We have been chasing this fugitive for a great deal of your time."

"What will he do if we don't agree to his challenge?" Laverne asked.

"More than likely flee, *after* doing some very permanent damage to your culture. A couple of those apples in the wrong hands would have a very destructive result on your young culture I am afraid."

Laverne glanced around at me. "Can you keep him playing long enough, Poker Boy?"

I glanced at the golden snake on the screen, then at Lady Luck. "I can, with a little help."

"Come in undetected," Laverne said, turning back to Commander. "Your fugitive will be waiting for you at a poker table in Las Vegas."

"Thank you," the big golden snake said, and the screen went dark.

I sure hated snakes.

Lady Luck turned to me. "What kind of help do you need?"

I glanced at Patty, then back at Laverne. "Can you, without Snake noticing, slow down the time in the casino while we play? Make the seventeen hours actually seem more like four or five? I can hold an all-in player for that long, but not a lot longer I'm afraid."

Laverne and Stan both nodded, clearly understanding what I was asking for. Patty just looked puzzled, so to make sure we were all on the same page, I explained to her what I was thinking.

"The Snake has nothing really to lose, so in a no-limit game, he can just shove in all his chips at any given point. Without me facing him in a one-hand showdown, he can just whittle me down slowly as I keep folding. My problem is that I don't dare win or lose. My assignment isn't to beat Snake, it is to play him for a long time, to a draw. Much, much harder thing to do."

"I get it," Patty said, nodding.

"Let's just hope he came to play," Stan said. "I'll set it up in a private room at the MGM. Give me five minutes."

With that Stan vanished.

"Good luck," Laverne said, her face tight and not smiling.

The big office of the head of all the Gambling Gods faded and Patty and I were left standing in the hallway outside of the MGM Grand poker room.

"I really hate it when Lady Luck wishes me good luck," I said, shaking my head.

"Yeah," Patty said. "That's got to worry you. Means she can't really help you much."

"Great," I said, taking a deep breath. I was used to winning, not playing someone to a draw.

"Ready," Stan said, appearing beside us. He indicated a door off to one side of the poker room.

Patty leaned over and kissed me on the cheek, which for a quick second made me forget about how much I hated snakes and remember how much I really liked her. "Luck," she said.

"It will be interesting, if nothing else," I said, smiling at her. I glanced at Stan. "Think you can slow things down a little?"

"We'll see what we can do," Stan said. "But if he starts to notice, we'll back off and you'll be on your own."

"Just keep the snake-bite kit handy," I said, then turned and walked toward the table where the alien sat.

Chapter Four

"Private room," I said as I got near the alien, indicating the door. "Chips are being set up. You have yourself a bet."

"Perfect," the alien said, smiling again, rustling his dry skin.

I indicated that the pit boss should cash in our real chips and bring them to us, then led the way into the private room.

A poker table filled the center of the meeting room, and a MGM Grand dealer was sitting ready. Two large stacks of chips of varied denominations were stacked in front of the third chair and the seventh chair, facing each other.

I indicated that Snake should pick and he took the three chair while I shut the door behind us.

I sat down and then pointed upward. "We're being

recorded and watched by two casino employees to ensure no problems."

"Understandable," he said. Then he smiled again and even from the length of the table I saw dandruff float down onto his narrow shoulders.

As Stan said, luckily, Snake had come to actually play. So, for the first hour, we traded hands back and forth, pretty much ending up level. I would raise and he would fold, he would raise and I would fold. We saw maybe a dozen flops total, with one or the other of us betting and the other folding. Not the kind of match the television folks would be happy with. In fact, on television, the first hour would mostly be edited right out.

I held a slight advantage of less than eighty thousand going into the second hour, not enough to count in this kind of game.

About ten minutes into the second hour, I caught a pair of kings on the button and raised it twenty thousand. Snake smiled and reraised another fifty. I smooth called and we went to the flop.

A third king hit the flop, but there was also an ace and ten, rainbow, meaning all suits.

Snake, with a rustling sound moved another fifty thousand into the pot.

A smallish bet, which might mean he wanted me to call. I didn't like the feel of it.

I sat back and stared at the board, trying my best to get a read on Snake's hand. More than likely he had aces and had me dead. I doubted he would have reraised with Jack/Queen to give him the straight. And if he had ace/king, I had him dead with two pair.

But the key was, I didn't want to win this pot. If I folded now, I would still be slightly ahead, but I had to fold perfectly, showing him I had a read on him, to keep him under control and playing light.

So, like any good poker player, I went into acting mode. I always figured there should be an Academy Award for poker table acting. Those of us who are pros can act with the best of them. It's also why some damn fine actors become good poker players. They already have part of the skill down solid.

"Let me see if I have this right," I said, smiling at Snake and leaning forward. "You reraised me before the flop, not large, but large enough. Now, with the ace on the board, you come out betting, again not huge, but strong enough to make it interesting. Why do I feel like I'm being suckered into this pot?"

He again lowered his sunglasses and I could see his dark eyes under the lip of his cowboy hat. "You trying to get a read on me, Poker Boy?"

I laughed. "Oh, I already have that," I lied. "You're sitting there with a pair of aces in your hand and trying to sucker me in like I'm one of those rank players out there. Maybe next time."

I flipped my pocket kings toward the dealer, face-up so he could see them.

He stared at my kings for a moment as the dealer scooped

them up and then the sound of snakeskin rustling filled the room. Oh, oh, I had made him mad. That snakebite kit might not be such a bad idea after all. I had been right about his aces.

He flipped his two cards to the dealer without showing them to me and started stacking the chips from the pot as the rustling slowly faded.

Why couldn't the aliens have been badgers, or gophers, or even alligators? Anything but snakes.

Chapter Five

For the next half hour, Snake shed a lot of dandruff and folded almost everything, and I gained chips on him, slowly working it up so that I had a couple hundred thousand extra on him, enough to fold some hands without being in any danger. If I hadn't been playing an alien snake, I would have said that my play had Snake snake-bit.

But I said nothing. I just hoped time outside of this room was moving a lot faster than it was in this room.

Finally, around the beginning of the second hour, Snake seemed to shake himself, a rustling sound that sent dandruff flying everywhere. I had no idea how much dandruff would be covering the table, the chips, everything, if he hadn't been wearing that cowboy hat. I just hoped the snake he made the cowboy hat from hadn't been a relative.

Or another poker player.

Two hands later, he raised and I folded.

For the next fifteen hands straight, he raised and I folded. He clearly had changed strategy and I was looking tight and weak to him with my play now.

"What's wrong, Poker Boy?" Snake asked as I folded yet another hand. "Afraid to play?"

"No cards," I again lied. Poker players lie a lot to other poker players. Actually, I had folded six perfectly playable hands to his raises. I just didn't see any point in mixing it up yet, since I was still a good hundred and fifty thousand ahead of him and was in no hurry at all.

Three more hands he raised and I folded, then with him raising ten thousand, I looked down and saw the worst hand in poker. Seven/deuce off-suit. So I reraised him fifty thousand.

He stared at me from behind those sunglasses, his face ringed with a coat of dandruff white, then finally folded.

I flipped my cards again face up so he could see my bluff. "Got tired of the bad cards. Decided to play a couple."

The rustling filled the room again and the dandruff flew as Snake shuddered and got even angrier. At this point, he had to know he was way outclassed in this game and that I had a complete read on him, even though I didn't really. One of two things would be his reaction. He would settle into slow, steady play, or he would get even more aggressive.

Luckily, after a small dandruff storm, he settled down and

stopped raising every hand, and we went back to exchanging blinds with small raises as we had done the first hour.

In that style of play, with me not having any ability to sense him at all, or his hands, he was dangerous in the long run. But it would take a long time for him to wear me down, and that's what I needed to have happen.

Finally, just under four hours into the game, we had a hand that television announcers would love. I had ace/queen and raised thirty thousand.

He flat called and we went to the flop. I put him on a pair, or maybe a weak ace such as ace/nine. At that point I was fairly certain we were going in mostly even.

Flop came out ace and two eights. I had two pair, aces and eights, but I didn't much like that flop.

He bet out forty thousand and this time I called him.

The next card was a third eight, filling me up. But again, I hated that card more than I wanted to admit. We were either going to tie if he also had an ace, or I was beat with my full house against his quads if he had the forth ace.

He checked.

I checked right behind him.

Dandruff flew, telling me he wanted me to bet. It seemed his tell was his bad skin problem. He had the eights.

The last card was a worthless rag, and he bet out another forty grand, just enough to keep me in. I called him, since I would still be up slightly even losing the pot, and he rolled over ace eight.

I rolled over my ace/queen and Snake said "Nice hand," as the dealer shoved him the chips."

"Nice bet," I said.

So after four hours of play, we were still almost even. So far, I had managed to do what I needed to do.

CHAPTER SIX

By the end of hour five, I was a hundred grand behind, all from small pots, and Snake's shirt was almost pure white from the dandruff.

By the end of hour six, I was two hundred thousand behind, and Snake had settled into the pattern that I knew from the beginning would wear me down. In a game where winning and losing were an option, I would have ended this hours ago. It had already gone on a lot longer than I had thought possible.

And I thought the same thing by the end of hour seven. I had pressured him into folding a few hands, being clear that he was beat, but he had gotten me to fold even more, and now my chips were just over six hundred thousand.

"Be nice to my chips," I said, smiling at him. "They are about to come back my way. I can feel the cards turning."

He just grinned and rustled his skin and shed even more dandruff. "We shall see, Poker Boy. We shall see."

My comment had the desired effect and he started raising regularly again, forcing his play, and for a good dozen hands, I folded everything, pretending to get angry at the cards for not turning, even though I was seeing some perfectly good playable hands.

Then, on the button, I looked down at pocket rockets. Two wonderful red aces.

"It's about damn time," I said, and raised a smooth forty thousand. My comment, of course, would tell any decent poker player I really *didn't* have a strong hand. He just called and sat back in his chair.

Not a good sign. He had a monster hand as well.

Flop came ace/queen/jack, rainbow. He bet out forty thousand, the same bet I had made and I flat called him with my three aces. And then I sat back.

"Interesting," Snake said, looking over the top of his sunglasses at me with his dark eyes.

I said nothing and the turn came a ten. If he had ace/king, he had just hit his straight and I was beat.

Before he could reach for his chips I said, "I wouldn't bet much on that straight until you see the river."

His hand froze over his chips, letting me know I had figured his hand perfectly. And by speaking up, I had told him exactly what I had as well. His straight was the best hand, but I had to get any one of one ace, three queens, three jacks, or three tens to win the hand and two kings to tie him with a straight of my own. Twelve outs were a lot of outs.

At that moment, a shimmering went through the air and I had the sense that a bunch of hours suddenly passed. The door to the room opened and two large, gold-colored, snake-like men walked through, followed by Laverne and Stan and Patty.

In a hissing language I had no desire to learn, the two golden-snake men moved over behind Snake and made him stand, sending dandruff everywhere like a faint snowstorm.

Snake glanced at the cards and then up at me. "Nicely played, Poker Boy. A match I will always remember."

"As will I," I said. But not because of the poker, but I didn't say that.

"Any chance we can see that river card?" Snake asked.

I nodded to the dealer and he flipped the last card over. Another ten.

I rolled over my aces full.

"I guess it wasn't meant to be," Snake said.

A moment later the three aliens vanished.

"Nice job, again, Poker Boy," Laverne said, smiling at me. Then she, too, vanished.

I can't begin to say, as a poker player, how much I liked having Lady Luck smile at me.

Stan smiled as well. "We owe you one for that." Then he was gone.

Patty kissed me, and for a second I forgot all about snakes, poker, and Lady Luck as I enjoyed the feel of Front Desk Girl welcoming me back to the real world.

"Have I ever told you," Patty said as we turned and headed for the door, "how much I hate snakes."

"Oh, after about five hours of playing poker with one, you get used to them."

She laughed. "You up for a wonderful dinner, on me?"

"I think I need a shower first," I said as we walked arm-in-arm down the hallway.

"Oh, I like that idea, too," Patty said, hugging me even closer. "I'll scrub."

"Only if you use a lot of shampoo," I said. "Dandruff shampoo."

Daddy Is An Undertaker

CHAPTER ONE

I usually find the people I'm going to help by accident. Most of us superheroes do, or we are told to help someone by one of our bosses. But this time, my sidekick and girlfriend, Patty Ledgerwood, aka Front Desk Girl brought me a person who really needed help.

And I do mean a lot of help if she planned on staying alive more than another few hours.

Actually, Patty sent my boss, Stan, the God of Poker, to get me.

It was a dark and rainy Oregon Saturday night in March. I was dressed and watching a rerun of an old Star Trek show starring the bald actor whose name I can never remember. In an hour or so, I planned on heading over to the casino near the doublewide trailer I called home. I never went near the casino too early on a weekend night, because the players were new and fresh and hadn't had enough drinks.

I always gave the Saturday players a few hours, and then went over to take the money that they were willing to give to me across the poker table. Even though I was a superhero, I still had to make a living, and playing poker was my way of doing it.

"Knock, knock. Poker Boy, need to talk," the voice-without-a-body said from the middle of the air in my living room, interrupting a scene with an alien with a forehead problem and some sort of sticky paste-like substance.

I knew the voice. Stan had only been to my home once before for only a second. It wasn't like him to be polite and actually knock.

"I'm decent," I said, standing and heading for my super-hero costume on the hook by the door. I had on tennis shoes, jeans, and a white Polo shirt, but my costume was my black leather coat and black Fedora-like hat that I never took off in a casino. It helped funnel the power of the casino to me. If Stan was coming to talk to me, I know I was going to need the costume very quickly.

Stan appeared in the middle of my living room and glanced first at the old television, then the remains of my T.V. dinner on the scarred coffee table, then around at the old 1970s furniture and green shag carpet that had come with the doublewide when it was new.

"We clearly don't pay you enough," Stan said, disgusted at what he saw.

"You don't pay me anything," I said as I slipped on my coat and hat.

"Oh, yeah, there's that," Stan said. "But I know for a fact you have enough in your bank accounts to buy a dozen mansions in every state in the country, with enough left over for a castle in Britain."

I shrugged. He was right. In about fifty accounts in fifty different banks, I had a vast amount of money. And a ton of investments that seemed to be doing real well when I bothered to check on them. I had won a lot of tournaments and just didn't spend much money after taxes every year.

"I like it here," I said. "Keeps me humble."

"Oh, yeah, Poker Boy humble," Stan said, laughing. "I bet Patty doesn't come over often,"

With that he had a point. We always stayed at her wonderful place in Vegas. She had only seen my home once and never come back. Maybe Stan was right, it might be time to upgrade some. When I had the time.

And besides, Patty thought I was a broke gambler. Maybe at some point I should get around to telling her about my money. Not a conversation I was looking forward to.

"So what do I owe this visit?" I asked the God of Poker.

"Just doing a favor for your girlfriend," Stan said. "She needs your help on a case and she asked me to come get you. Guess there isn't enough time for you to fly commercial." Stan just shook his head at my old doublewide. "You know, you could afford a few private jets as well."

"Or you could teach me the jumping-around-in-space skill," I said. "Or is that only for Gods?"

He shrugged. "Maybe when you're done helping Patty."

I was actually surprised at that. I didn't know I might be able to actually teleport around the world. Of course, I still didn't know what half my powers were. I was still pretty new at this superhero stuff.

The next moment I was in the crowded lobby of the MGM Grand.

The noise of the casino and the hundreds of guests in the lobby slammed into me. But at the same time I could feel the energy coming from the casino through my coat and hat, making me feel extra alive.

Patty was standing in front of the desk, talking to a woman with longish blonde hair. Patty glanced over, saw me, and smiled.

Like normal, her smile melted a part of me and got other parts all agitated in a very good way. She had the ability to do that to me with just a look. Her long brown hair was pulled back and she was dressed in the standard MGM front desk uniform of white shirt and black slacks and MGM vest. She made it look great.

She was a stunningly attractive woman. What she saw in me was anyone's guess.

I made my way through the crowd and luggage over to her and she gave me a hug. "Thanks for coming."

"Anytime," I said, and I meant it.

"Thanks, Stan," Patty said to the air.

"More than welcome," Stan said without showing himself.

The young woman with Patty sort of looked around for the voice, but before she could say anything Patty said, "Lisa, this is Poker Boy."

I turned on my what I called my "Charming Power" for lack of a better name. It helped put people I was trying to help in a more relaxed and talkative mood. I shook her firm hand. "Very nice meeting you."

Lisa looked like an odd imitation of an American flag, with a red, white and blue outfit that included a too-tight skirt. It really wasn't a flattering look on her. Up close I could tell she couldn't be more than twenty-two, and more than likely she would get carded everywhere she went in this town.

Plus she had on way too much makeup. Her eyelashes seemed to extend halfway into the big lobby.

She smiled, but the smile didn't reach her dark eyes. I could tell that something was very wrong in her life.

"Tell him what's bothering you," Patty said, patting Lisa's arm gently in support.

As a superhero in the world of hospitality, Patty could calm the most upset person and make them feel good about anything. It was one of her many superpowers.

Lisa nodded, took a deep breath, and then in a deep southern accent she said, "My daddy is an undertaker."

I waited for her to keep going, but she seemed to think that was enough explanation of her problem.

Finally I said, "Yes, go on. What's happening?"

"No, you don't see do you?" Lisa said, clearly about to break into tears that I was sure would run black from all the makeup. "I'm turning twenty-one in four hours, and my daddy is an undertaker."

I looked puzzled and was about to try a tell-me-the-truth power on her when Patty said softly to me, "Capitalize the word *Undertaker*."

I opened my mouth to say something, then the realization hit me: the young woman in front of me was the child of an *Undertaker*, the most feared branch of all the deities.

That wasn't possible.

Undertakers never had children.

I had never heard of an Undertaker having a kid, and of all the rumors about Undertakers, the worst rumor was that their kids never lived past the first moment of their twenty-first birthday!

Now I saw the problem.

"Which one of the twelve is your father?" I asked softly, almost afraid to hear the answer. There were only twelve, one per month. It seems the twelve of them took turns being Death for the month.

"They call him Mortuary Dan," Lisa said.

Patty's face went white, and I felt like the chicken TV dinner I had eaten was about to make another showing in the lobby of the MGM Grand.

"I'm assuming you want to live longer than four more hours?" I asked, getting right to the point as I tried to get my stomach back under control.

The worst part of the kid rumor was that their own fathers took them.

The Undertakers took everyone at one point or another, except for maybe the Gods, who seemed to live a very long time. And some superheroes as well. Patty had been a superhero for about a hundred years before I became one. I'm not aging now and so far we've never talked much about what happened in those hundred years before I was born.

"I would like to live longer," she said. "Much longer. Can you help me?"

Usually I just say that I can help the person, give them encouragement, make them feel something positive. But all I said to Lisa was, "We can try."

But what Patty and I could do against an Undertaker was beyond me. Especially Mortuary Dan, the oldest of all the Undertakers. He was the worst, the nastiest of the twelve from what I had heard. All twelve were nasty people. Dealing with the dead and dying every day, day after day, would do that to a person. It was no wonder they only worked one month at a time. I had no idea what they did the other eleven months of the year. I honestly didn't want to know.

Somehow, to save this woman, we had to stop Death himself.

The big problem was that Death was her father.

Chapter Two

I took a deep breath and tried to pull my thoughts together. Somehow, we had to stop the tradition of not letting a child of an Undertaker live longer than the first moment of their twenty-first birthday.

I had no idea at all why such a stupid rule existed.

"Has your father ever talked to you about this?" I asked Lisa.

She shook her head.

"Do you have a place to stay here in Vegas?" I asked.

Lisa nodded. "I came here to enjoy my last night, then when checking in, I broke down in front of Patty and told her the entire story."

"Tell you what, Lisa, go ahead and go to your room, have a nice relaxing bath, then meet us down here in two hours if we haven't contacted you first. We need to do some work and you might as well enjoy the time it's going to take us."

"I'll upgrade you to a nice suite," Patty said, nodding to me and gently turning Lisa around toward the front desk before the Daughter of Death could object.

I pulled out my phone and called Screamer and had him meet us at our normal place downtown in fifteen minutes. Then I called The Smoke, the fourth member of my team, a human who could turn into a wolf when he wanted. He was out of town and working a case in the Canadian woods. There was no way he could make it in time, and I could tell he felt bad. I assured him that missing this one was a very good idea.

Then, as Patty got Lisa headed toward the elevators and turned to join me, I shouted into the noise and crowds of the large lobby, "Stan! Need some help!"

Around me the room froze except for Patty, as Stan took us out of time and appeared beside me. Everyone else just stopped in the instant of time. I had the power to do that as well, but Stan was better at it than I was.

"I thought I might be getting a call when I saw who needed help. You know the rumor is that she's going to be dead in a few hours by her own father's hand."

"That's what we need help with. We want to try to stop that."

Stan just laughed long and hard, choking before catching his breath. His laugh echoed in the quiet of the frozen huge lobby.

Patty and I didn't join him.

After a moment he said, "You two are serious, aren't you?"

Patty and I both nodded. "I don't even understand why a rule like that exists," I said.

"Because it does," Stan said.

"Why?" Patty asked. "How did it get started? Maybe if we knew that, we might be able to figure a way around it."

Stan shrugged. "I honestly don't know. It's just been a rule for the few children of Undertakers for as long as I have been around. Although, to be honest, no Undertaker has had a child except for Lisa in all my years. She's the only one."

I wanted to ask Stan how long that was, but decided it was a question for another time.

"Would Laverne know the reason behind all of this?" I asked, not really believing I had asked that question. Laverne was Lady Luck herself, one of the most powerful of all the gods. Patty and Screamer and I had saved her once, but that doesn't mean lowly superheroes like me and Patty and Screamer can bother her at every whim. But I was hoping that Stan might ask Burt, the God of Casino Operations; and if he didn't know, maybe Burt would ask Lady Luck.

"I don't know if she does or not," Stan said. "You meeting the rest of your team at The Diner?"

I nodded. "The Smoke is busy in Canada, but Screamer will be there."

"I'll see what I can do," Stan said. "I'll meet you at The Diner as soon as I get some information. You know, you two worry me sometimes, screwing with things you shouldn't screw with."

Both of us nodded at that. What could we say?

He vanished, letting us slip back into normal time as he did. Around us the movement and the noise filled the air again, slamming around us like a stream moving around rocks.

"Sorry to get you into this," Patty said, looking worried as we turned and headed for the parking garage.

"Any excuse to spend time with you is great by me."

She laughed. "Silly, you never need an excuse, you know that."

For a moment I actually forgot that we were going up against an Undertaker, Death himself, to try to save Death's daughter.

Chapter Three

Fifteen minutes later I told the problem to Screamer, a superhero with the power to read other people's minds and transfer thoughts.

We were sitting at a large table in The Diner, a hole-in-the-wall little restaurant decorated with pretend 1960s stuff. It was on a side street downtown, and a woman named Madge was our normal waitress. She always wore her uniform three sizes too small, and it was a chore to not stare when she had to pick anything up.

If you *did* stare, you ended up having nightmares for a week about exploding humans. Or at least I always did.

We had started going to The Diner when the team first formed and we had to fight the Slots of Saturn. And for every mission since, we met here to talk and plan and drink the fantastic milkshakes.

Madge had just sat down our milkshakes when Screamer said he was very worried about even thinking of going up against an Undertaker. "Superheroes can live a long time, but we do die. We can be killed."

That was a thought I didn't want to think about at all.

Suddenly the sounds from the street stopped, and Madge froze in mid-stride back toward the lunch counter in the back.

A moment later Laverne showed up with thin man dressed only in a loud-colored bathing suit and a white towel. I had no idea who he was, but he wasn't looking happy.

Stan appeared a moment later, smiled a sheepish grin, and sat down without a word at a nearby table to watch the fireworks.

"You know, Laverne," the man said, "I could have gotten at least two more waves in before sunset."

"Sorry, Dan," Laverne said, shaking her head.

Dan's bathing suit changed to a dark, silk business suit with his tie perfectly in place and a blue shirt under it that seemed like it belonged on a surfer.

Then Laverne said, "But after the month is over, you're going to have a lot of time to surf all you want."

Dan smiled, and an image of a skeleton face sort of flashed over his face. "You got that right."

All three of us at the table had slid back away from the front edge where Laverne and Dan were pulling up chairs and talking. I had zero doubt I was about to meet the most feared Undertaker of them all, Mortuary Dan.

Dan sat down and then glanced at us, nodding. "I see,

Laverne, that you have your top superhero team together here, minus one. What can I do to help?"

Laverne glanced at the milkshake in front of Patty.

Patty nodded that it was all right for Laverne to take a drink and slid it to Lady Luck. After a sip, Laverne smiled, then turned to Dan with a serious expression. "You need to talk to your daughter."

"Why?" Dan asked. "I'm going to see her in just under four hours."

Wow, this guy was cold, even for Death.

"She doesn't know what's going to happen," Laverne said.

"That's silly," Dan said, taking Screamer's untouched milkshake and sipping it. "Wow! These are darned fine milkshakes. I can see why you guys meet here."

I think I nodded, but damned if I was going to say anything.

"She doesn't know, Dan," Laverne said, again sipping on the milkshake. "All she knows is the rumors handed down over centuries. You know she's the first kid of any Undertaker since the Dark Ages."

Dan nodded and made a large dent in the milkshake. "Yeah, those were tough times. It's been easier since."

The four of us just sat and listened to the two major gods talk and drink our milkshakes. As superheroes, what else could we do?

"She thinks she's going to die," Laverne said.

"Technically, she is," Dan said, slurping the milkshake and somehow managing to not get any on his silk suit.

"She contacted Poker Boy and his team to try to figure out a way to stop it."

Dan sat the milkshake glass down hard, then turned and looked me directly in the eye. His face seemed to flash back and forth between skin and skeleton, and it had to be the most frightening thing I had ever seen. "What do you say to her?"

I sputtered, then dug down and managed to apply some calming skills from my years playing poker and said, "We told her we would find out what was happening."

He looked at me for a moment, than shook his head. "You don't know either, do you?"

Laverne laughed. "Dan, remember how long it has been since any of you had a kid. None of the younger superheroes or gods know anything more than the tradition of Undertakers killing their children."

He looked at Laverne, then back at me and my team. "So you are telling me, Lisa doesn't know what's going to happen in a few hours?"

"She believes she's going to die, sir," I said. "She's terrified."

Dan slammed his fist on the table, rocking all the milkshake glasses. If we hadn't been between time and frozen, that would have brought Madge running.

Dan's face went to complete skeleton, then he pushed his chair back and stood. "I knew I shouldn't have trusted her mother to raise her."

I desperately wanted to ask who Lisa's mother was, but

smartly kept my mouth shut. When Death himself was pissed off, making him even angrier wasn't a good plan toward a long life.

Mortuary Dan paced for a moment, and even Laverne let him go, drinking the rest of Patty's milkshake with a slight smile on her face.

Finally Dan stopped and turned back to the table. "Anyone have any ideas what I should do?"

I didn't have a clue what the problem was, other than the legend that he had to kill his daughter in a few hours – and he didn't seem to be denying that at all.

I glanced at Patty. Her face was white and she was leaning back toward me. Screamer just seemed stunned.

Stan, in the other booth, had his God of Poker face on, and I couldn't even begin to get a read on what he was thinking or feeling.

"You need to talk to your daughter," Laverne said softly. "Before midnight. She needs to know and understand what's going to happen."

"Oh," Dan said, clearly disgusted as he started to pace again. "She's going to be so scared of me now, she won't listen. And she needs to know."

"Yes, she does," Laverne said, her voice softer and more compassionate than I had ever heard from Lady Luck.

I wanted to raise my hand like a kid in class and ask just what the adults in the room were talking about, but again my common sense got the best of me and I kept my mouth shut.

Dan kept pacing, clearly thinking, and after a moment

Laverne looked over at me and Patty and Screamer. "I think Dan needs your help," she said.

Okay, at that moment you could have knocked me down with a slight breeze. Lady Luck just told us that Death needed our help.

Dan stopped and stared at the table, clearly as puzzled as I was, which made me feel only a slight bit better.

"Can you four," Laverne asked, nodding to us and Stan, "get Lisa and bring her here and help her father tell her what is going to happen tonight? She needs to be kept calm. Very calm."

Laverne just stared at me and Patty. After a moment we both nodded, starting to understand what we needed to do.

"And she needs to learn vast amounts of information from her father in a very short time." She glanced at Screamer who just turned white at the idea.

"I see where you are going, Laverne," Dan said, stepping back to the table and looking at me and my team. "Would you help me help my daughter through the transition?"

I couldn't take it any longer, I had to ask something, so I asked the most pressing question of the thousands I had spinning in my mind.

"What transition?"

"At midnight," Dan said, "Lisa will change from being a mere mortal to being an immortal God. An Undertaker. I'm retiring to surf in Hawaii. She's taking my spot, the first female Undertaker. I start her training at midnight tonight."

CHAPTER FOUR

In my few short years of being a superhero, I had never been so scared of an assignment. Somehow the three of us, with Stan's help, needed to link up a god, Death himself, and his daughter in an out-of-time link so that he could have the time to talk to her. And we needed to help her understand what was coming, and that it was all right that she was going to die.

Or sort of die, anyway.

If we screwed this up, none of us might live to see the end of the year.

If that long.

I had a hunch Mortuary Dan wouldn't think twice about just moving us on to the next place, wherever or whatever that was.

Stan gave me and Patty a lift to pick up Lisa.

When we appeared in her suite, she was still dressed in the same red, white, and blue outfit and was sitting on the couch. Clearly she had been sitting there since she arrived.

When she saw us, she jumped and rolled up over the back of the couch to get it between her and us.

I glanced at Patty. "She doesn't know anything at all about Gods and Superheroes, does she?"

"Not much I discovered," Patty said.

"How did you do that?" Lisa asked.

"I've been wondering the same thing," I said, glancing at Stan, who just shrugged. "We've got some good news for you," I continued, as Patty and I started working to calm her down with all the calming powers we had between us.

"You do?" she asked, clearly relaxing and even starting to smile, forgetting that we had just appeared out of nowhere in front of her.

"You're not going to die at midnight," I said, fibbing a little. She actually wasn't going to die. She just wasn't going to be mortal anymore.

A slight detail.

"But there's one condition," Patty said. "You need to talk to your dad. And your dad wants us there with you for support."

Lisa started shaking her head back and forth and I could feel the panic starting to gain intensity.

I dug deep and Patty and I joined hands and hit her with every calming power we had. And I have to say, that was considerable. We could have put a bull moose to sleep.

Lisa calmed some.

"It's only to talk," I said. "He needs to tell you where the rumor is coming from and why it exists. He said your mother should have taught you all of this."

"All she said was that my daddy is an Undertaker – the Grim Reaper."

"Well, he sort of is," I said. "And a pretty fine surfer, from what I gather."

"My father surfs?" Lisa asked, calming even more under the intense push of calming powers from me and Patty.

"Eleven months a year that's about all he does," Patty said, smiling.

Lisa finally stopped shaking her head and stared first at me, then at Stan. "Who exactly are you people?"

"I am known as Poker Boy. I am at the rank of superhero in the Gambling Gods universe, which basically means I do a lot of the chores the gods don't want to do."

She nodded, so I went on.

"This is Patty, also known as Front Desk Girl. She is a superhero working for the Gods of Hospitality."

I pointed at Stan. "This is my direct boss, Stan, the God of Poker. It is our boss, Lady Luck, known as Laverne, who convinced your father that he needed to talk to you and help you understand this different world before anything could happen tonight."

"But I still might die tonight?" Lisa said, the panic starting to build again even against the onslaught of calming that Patty and I were directing toward her.

"Oh, trust me," I said, "at ten minutes after midnight tonight ,you'll be talking to me just fine. And you could talk to me any time you wanted after that. I promise."

"As do I," Patty said, nodding. "You just need to have a conversation with your father first, to understand everything that's going on."

Lisa clearly calmed with our promise. Then she laughed. "My mom hated what my dad did for a living, and never wanted him to come around. And she said his world was full of nutcakes. If I believe who you say you are, I guess she was right."

"Oh, trust me," I said, "as a person fairly new to this world as well, it's crazier than you can even imagine."

Lisa smiled and took a deep breath. "All right, let's go see my father."

A moment later the four of us were standing in The Diner.

Both Dan and Laverne were halfway through two more milkshakes, sitting in the both with Screamer sitting in the middle looking slightly panicked. Madge was moving around, shaking her head as she sometimes did when she had to wait on us.

Mortuary Dan stood, his human face staying firmly in place, and stepped toward his daughter. "Hi, Lisa. It's wonderful to see you again. You've become a beautiful woman."

Lisa smiled and stepped into the hug of Death. "Hi, Daddy."

Chapter Five

We let Lisa and her father talk.

After a few minutes, Dan turned to all of us, with Madge standing right there beside the table. "We need to start all this. Lisa has a lot to learn about her old man. Madge, would you put up the closed sign and keep those milkshakes coming for all of us? To do this right, we're going to need the energy."

Madge nodded. "I'll be glad to, Dan. Lisa, what kind do you like?"

"Chocolate," Lisa said.

"You got it, dear," Madge said, turning to close the front door as Patty and Screamer and I stared.

"Madge is a superhero in Food and Beverage," Laverne said, clearly trying not to laugh. "I thought you all knew that."

I shook my head and glanced around at Stan, who just smiled and shrugged. He had known, just hadn't bothered to tell any of the rest of us.

Laverne took one more long drink from her milkshake, then stood. "I'll be back a little later."

She vanished leaving us all alone with Mortuary Dan and his daughter.

Dan pointed to the spot where Screamer sat in the back of the booth. "Poker Boy, you and Patty sit back there. Lisa, you sit on one side of the booth, I'll sit facing you so we can talk directly, and Screamer, you sit on a chair at the head of the booth so you can touch both of us."

Dan glanced over at Stan. "Keep us out of time for about forty-five minutes the first time. We'll adjust from there. And help everyone with energy when needed."

Stan nodded.

I thought my heart was going to pound out of my chest. In the back of the restaurant Madge had the milkshake blenders going full speed, filling the restaurant with the whining sound. It didn't begin to cover the sound of my heart.

I could feel Lisa suddenly starting to get upset again, so Patty and I both sent calming powers at her as we slid into position, our legs touching for extra support.

I don't know how we could calm anyone down, as worried as we were ourselves, but for some reason our calming powers weren't hooked to how we were feeling. Luckily.

"What's going to happen?" Lisa asked, clearly afraid to take her position in the booth.

"Screamer here is going to hook our thoughts up so I can help you learn faster all the things your mother didn't teach you over the last twenty-plus years. And that way you can get to know me, the real me."

"You can do that?" Lisa asked, staring at Screamer.

"I can," he said, turning to face where she stood. "It's my power. You can trust me, it will be painless. Odd and a little confusing at times, but painless, I promise you. It will be exactly as your dad said, and the connection help you learn very quickly what is a rumor and what is the truth."

"And I will be very careful to ease you into all of this," Dan said.

I was very glad he said that. I couldn't imagine suddenly knowing all at once all the things I had learned in my short five years being a superhero. But Lisa had no choice. She had to learn a lot and very quickly. There was only three hours to go until midnight.

"Ready, daughter?" Dan asked, smiling, and not showing his skeleton face at all.

Patty and I hit her with as much calming as we dared, and Lisa nodded. Then she slowly slid into position beside me in the booth.

I scooted closer to Patty to make sure I wasn't touching Lisa. Last thing I wanted to do was be included in the conversation they would have in their heads while Screamer held them together. But if I touched her, I would be automatically included, just as if Patty touched Dan on the other side.

The booth suddenly felt very, very small.

"I guess so," Lisa said.

Dan glanced at us and nodded, then nodded to Screamer.

Patty and I ramped up every bit of calming we could as Stan dropped us between time, killing all the sound in the restaurant and from the streets.

Screamer touched Lisa, then laid a hand gently on Mortuary Dan's arm.

For a moment, I thought we were going to have to calm Screamer down as well; but then he nodded and sat back and closed his eyes.

Lisa's eyes got huge and she was fidgeting some. I motioned for Stan to help, and he boosted both Patty's and my calming power.

Lisa calmed slightly. I was stunned she wasn't so calm she was asleep. The women had a very, very powerful mind. No wonder Laverne wanted us all to help Dan with this.

And why Dan wanted the help. He and Laverne both knew how powerful the child of a god would be to deal with.

Screamer kept his eyes closed, and Dan and Lisa just stared at each other. I slowly motioned for Stan to back off and he did, then Patty and I pulled back slightly, only increasing when we could sense Lisa getting upset.

Forty-five minutes later in out-of-time time, Stan said, "Break."

Screamer pulled his hands away and Stan dropped the

room back into real time. The sounds of Madge working on the milkshakes hit all of us hard.

Patty and I kept our concentration firmly on Lisa, who seemed to close her eyes, then open them and look at her father again as if she was seeing him for the first time.

No one said a word.

Then Lisa said, "So I'm not going to die, I'm going to become immortal at midnight."

Dan nodded. "For all intents and purposes, yes."

Lisa nodded, then said, "I have to use the restroom."

"I'll go with you," Patty said.

And wow was I glad she said that, since I had no idea how I was going to make it through more hours without visiting the restroom myself.

"I'll be right back," Dan said and vanished.

Stan also vanished.

"You all right?" I asked Screamer. I had no idea what it would be like inside of Death's mind, and I was very glad I didn't have to find out.

"I'm fine, actually. Dan is keeping me and Lisa blocked from most of his mind, just showing Lisa what she needs to see to get started. But this isn't going to be a short process."

"That slow?" I asked.

He nodded. Then he and I both headed for the rest rooms in the back, meeting Madge with a tray full of shakes.

"Don't tell me you all are leaving again?" she asked.

"Just a break," I said. "But I have a hunch that by the time this is over, you're going to wish we had left."

"Anything going on with both Laverne and Mortuary Dan, I suppose you might be right."

She went to put our milkshakes on the table as I just kept on, shaking my head at all the surprises I was getting on a simple Saturday night.

CHAPTER SIX

It took nine hours of actual lesson time spread over six different sessions in just over three hours of real time before Lisa finally seemed to know what she was getting into and was ready.

It was five minutes until midnight.

Patty and I had stopped helping keep Lisa calm about three lessons back. Stan had asked me on the last break to help him keep up the out-of-time shield, since he was getting tired and Screamer needed some help with energy as well from him.

So for most of the last hour of lesson time, with Stan spelling me every ten minutes, I held up the shield that kept us out of real time.

As we dropped back into real time and Screamer moved away from the two he had kept connected for almost nine hours, everyone climbed out of the booth. I felt as if I had sat in that booth for most of my life.

Laverne appeared, smiling. She and Dan moved off to one side for a moment as Patty and I stayed with Lisa.

"Amazing stuff I was born into," Lisa said. "I wish someone had told me about this last year so I wouldn't have been so worried for so long, but thanks to all of you, this didn't catch me by surprise now."

"Good," Patty said. "Knowledge is far, far more powerful than rumors."

"But only slightly less scary," Lisa said.

Suddenly, around the restaurant, other people began to pop in, almost none of them anyone I knew, until the place was very crowded with only an open circle in the middle of the floor where a table used to be.

Stan stepped over beside us and whispered. "The other eleven Undertakers have arrived, plus a number of top gods from all the deities. This is a real event."

Stan and Screamer and Patty and I sort of moved back against the edge of the booth to allow the really powerful to take their places around the center.

"Are you ready to join me, daughter?" Dan asked, stepping into the circle in center of the crowd.

Lisa smiled at us, then turned and stepped forward. "I am."

"Thirty seconds," Laverne said.

Dan indicated that Lisa should kneel in front of him and she did.

"Thank you all for joining this special occasion," Dan said, his face now a complete skeleton, even though his hands and business suit looked perfectly pressed and in order. "We are here to welcome to our ranks the first new Undertaker in centuries. And the first woman to ever hold that position."

"Five seconds," Laverne said.

Dan reached out both hands and placed them over Lisa's head. Then as the clock ticked midnight, Lisa seemed to slump slightly, then something bright and shining and very yellow filled the air around her.

After a moment the yellow light all went inside of her, like she was a giant sponge soaking up water.

After a long pause, she opened her eyes and smiled.

Everyone cheered.

I didn't know what to think. I don't think I could feel so relieved in all my life.

"May I introduce you to the newest god?" Dan said, extending an arm to his daughter to help her off her knees. "My daughter Lisa. An Undertaker."

The entire room cheered, then calmed as Lisa looked around, smiling, nodding at many people she now clearly knew somehow.

Then she looked at us and said simply, "Thank you, Poker Boy, Screamer, Stan, and Patty. And most of all Laverne, who loaned my father such a wonderful team to help me through this transition. I will be forever grateful to you all."

Everyone cheered.

And I did as well, and just kept smiling.

Somehow we had managed to save yet another person. And that always felt great.

But it felt even better to have Death herself grateful to you.

It just didn't get any better than that.

GAMBLING HELL

CHAPTER 1

The ten-twenty hold'em game at the Mirage was going just fine until Heidi sat down in the empty seat.

I was up about three hundred and enjoying the game, staying out of the way of another pro at the other end of the table. We were basically taking turns slowly relieving the tourists of their money, while making sure they had a good time giving it to us.

Heidi, with her long blonde hair, plunging v-neck sweater, and front-loaded assets shifted the feeling of the table. I sensed it at once, even without using my Ultra-Intuitive Super Power.

She gave everyone a bright, white smile, fumbled with her chips like she was a beginner, and then laughed at something the tourist beside her said that more than likely wasn't funny.

At once my Poker Boy Gut-Sense Power shouted at me like a voice coming up from the depths of the Grand Canyon. Normally the power never shouted at me unless I asked it to. Now the Gut-Sense Grand Canyon voice was echoing in my head.

She's a good player!

The breasts are fake!

She's evil!

As the superhero Poker Boy, I've fought my share of evil and played with more than my share of both good and bad poker players. The first because fighting evil is what super-heroes do. It is the job description. The second because I make my living, pay the expenses to the next fight against evil, by playing professional poker.

Trust me, superheroes have to get money somewhere, and it might as well be from people who are enjoying themselves over a card game while they gave me money to cover the costs of fighting those that needed to be fought.

Since the first day I put on my leather coat and Fedora-like hat that became my superhero costume, I knew that the Gambling Gods ran anything to do with gambling. Laverne, Lady Luck herself, was head of all things corporate, with Burt the General Manager running all casino operations in the god realm.

Stan was the main God of Poker and my direct boss. I liked Stan, and over the years I had actually met both Laverne and Burt during adventures. I knew them to be powerful and damned scary. No poker player I know of screws around with

Lady Luck and lives to win another pot. I always treated Laverne with the respect she deserved and so far my luck had just been fine.

Of course, over the years there had always been evil to fight. Otherwise there would have been no need for my services as Poker Boy. But until Heidi sat down at my table, I had never faced evil over a game. And I had no real understanding that there was also a gambling hell where the evil I was fighting came from.

To be honest, I'm not sure why I hadn't put two and two together and come up with a gambling hell. The evil had to come from somewhere, didn't it? Besides, if there were Gambling Gods, I knew there had to be a gambling hell to keep the universe balanced. I just hadn't thought of it before I met the denizen of Gambling Hell named Heidi.

She had finished stacking her chips in a beginner-like manner, a neat triangle coming out from the rail, all chips stacked neatly in piles of five. Then she looked up at me and smiled.

Only there was nothing about that smile that reached her dark eyes.

I didn't move, didn't smile back, but it was clear from her look that she knew who I was.

And she was challenging me.

My Grand Canyon warning voice echoed in my head again.

EVIL!

Evil!

evil!

After the echo in my head died off, my next thought was to rack up my chips and just find another table, or maybe even call it a night. But I was a superhero, and superheroes didn't run from evil, they fought it, head on. Normally I had to go track it down, dig it out, and then vanquish it in some fashion or another. Evil had very seldom come to me and asked to be beaten like Heidi was doing.

But now Evil itself was sitting three chairs down the table from me in a ten-twenty game, directly across from the dealer, and I had no idea why. But I had a hunch I was about to find out.

The pro at the other end of the table, a man I respected for his great skill at poker and his ability to read just about any player, gave Heidi a quick once-over, shook his head, and racked up his chips. He knew, just as I did, that what had been a very good game had just gone sour.

"Good luck," he said to me before turning to leave.

I nodded at him and then glanced down at the two cards the dealer had just given me. Pocket kings.

I was two in front of the blinds so I raised the bet to twenty. Everyone at the table folded except Heidi, who pretended to fumble with her chips and had to have the dealer help her get her bet right.

She was good. Every man at the table was watching her, either her smooth-skinned hands or her plunging neck-line.

The flop gave me another king, with two smaller cards that didn't match in suit or reach for a straight. Since I figured she was going to play the dumb blonde to the hilt and if I checked, she would check, I decided instead to bet ten more.

She again made a production out of calling. She was either giving me the first hand as part of the act, or she had aces and was playing me, pretending she didn't know what she was doing.

Then I realized there was something else going on. The calm, fun nature of the table was gone, replaced with tension and a focus that was distracted from the cards. It was almost as if the entire table had been shifted slightly out of the big Mirage Casino card room and into another dimension.

I glanced around. The rest of the room seemed distant and a little fuzzy.

So she wasn't just after the money, she was taking the table for another reason. As Poker Boy, I had seen a lot stranger things and for the moment I was willing to ride along to see exactly where we were going.

And why.

CHAPTER 2

The turn came another garbage card, with a rainbow, all four suits, on the board. I still had my three kings, but this time I just checked to her, wanting to see how she played her hand next. To a pro, in certain circumstances, a check means a weak hand. At other times it's a trap, meaning the hand is strong and the pro wants someone to bet so the pro can raise.

She looked at me with a puzzled smile on her face, pretending she didn't know what a check meant.

"Up to you," the young dealer said, resting his hand in front of the woman to indicate it was her turn to bet.

"Oh, it's my turn?" Heidi said, looking down at her cards again, then pretending to study the cards on the table. Then she looked up at the dealer, "What can I bet?"

A few men around the table who were taken in by her act

chuckled. When a beginning player asked how much they could bet, it always meant they had a strong hand, or thought they had a strong hand. With Heidi I knew it was all an act.

But with that question, the room around us seemed to grow even more distant and blurry. The noise from the other tables faded farther into the background.

I had a sense of downward movement. No one else at the table noticed, including the dealer, as all their attention remained focused on Heidi, her blonde hair, and her v-neck sweater.

"The bet is twenty," the dealer said.

She fumbled with her chips and then slid twenty forward.

She smiled at the dealer and then looked my way.

I knew I was going to have to make my move pretty soon to stop what she was doing with this table, but I wanted to see that last card before I did. If she had two aces in her hand, there were still two aces left out, and I wanted to be sure that third ace didn't hit the board before I moved. So I simply flat-called her twenty.

The dealer patted the table to indicate the bets were all square, burnt a card and turned over the river card. A four of hearts that matched the four of clubs already on the board.

I had kings full of fours, the highest full house possible with the cards on the board. But not the highest hand possible. And that worried me a lot.

Around the table the rest of the Mirage poker room had become nothing more than a distant blur, the only sounds a faint rumbling. And the air was getting warmer and warmer by the moment. Heidi was moving the entire game into gambling hell, and no one but me seemed to be noticing.

I took a deep breath and focused on a spot between two upcoming seconds. I wanted to use what I had called my Unstuck-in-Time power. Stan the God of Poker had told me I had the power, and since then it had come in handy more than once.

My power froze everyone's movements except Heidi. Clearly my power hadn't worked on her. She truly was evil and very powerful.

Seven of the men were frozen staring at her chest, the dealer and one of the other players were staring at her hands.

"Nice trick," she said, laughing in a way that made me shiver, even though I had on a leather jacket and the temperature around the table had gone up by twenty degrees.

By slipping myself between moments in time, I could see a little better where we were.

Granted, the Mirage Poker room was a faint overlay, sort of blurred and fuzzy, but through that vision I could clearly see a huge cave with dark walls and bright lights hanging from the roof. The table I was at seemed to be up near the roof of the cavern, still sitting in the Mirage, but yet at the same time floating in space, not yet all the way down to the surface.

A river of molten lava ran through one side of the cavern, accounting for the extra heat. There had to be at least a hundred different poker games going on around the room, all frozen because I was looking at them from a moment between seconds.

A poker room in gambling hell. This was the last place I wanted to be.

"So, Poker Boy," she said, smiling at me, "you hoping to freeze time and come and take a quick glance at what I have in my hand?"

I laughed at her. "Not my style. That's something you'd do I'm sure. I just wanted to stop this little elevator act you have going on."

"And you think this trick is going to stop it for long?" she asked, flaunting her chest assets by learning forward and making sure her v-neck sweater bagged out just enough.

Granted, I was a man. But I had turned down sexual advances from a goddess far more interesting than her, so her attempts to distract me dropped short.

"Long enough to get this settled," I said.

"And just how do you plan to settle this?" she asked, smiling at me. "Knock me off my chair?"

I stared at her, looking deep into her eyes. In my years of doing superhero deeds, I had found many ways of solving problems, and none of them, not once, had I needed to use any physical-type action. Anyone who actually looked at me would know I wouldn't be any good at that stuff anyway. I kept my poker face on and just kept staring at her, trying to get any kind of read on what exactly what would work. Frighteningly enough, at the moment I didn't know. I was just playing a bluff.

Chapter 3

She waved her arm around at the cavern. "You're in my world now."

I said nothing.

She shifted slightly, still smiling at me, still learning forward trying to get me to look at her fake assets.

I just stared at her face, into her eyes, like I stared at any poker player who tried to make a move on me. And I made sure I kept us firmly planted between seconds of time.

After a long moment of me staring at her she shifted slightly again, then turned to stare back, her fake smile frozen on her face.

I could tell I was getting to her. But I still had no idea what to do to get this table and all the men around it back into the Mirage poker room. I needed some answers.

"So what do you want me for?" I asked. "Why these guys?"

"Customers," she said. "Got to keep the operation running."

"No winning allowed down there," I said, indicating the tables frozen below us in the cavern.

She smiled again, and for the first time the smile reached her dark eyes. "Never."

Right at that moment I knew I had her. Just like I did in any tournament before making an all-in bet, I went quickly back over what had gone on before.

She'd been pulling a scam on the first hand after sitting down, and had gotten impatient to take the table down into her own world. And I'm sure there was a reason she was impatient.

Then I realized why. If we had reached the floor of the cavern in hell, I'm sure I would have lost the hand we were playing. She would have been able to change her cards into pocket fours, giving her quad fours, the only cards that would beat my kings-full in this hand. That's why she was in a hurry to get the table down. She wasn't used to losing and she was going to lose the first hand.

But we hadn't reached the floor of the cavern yet. And I could still see the Mirage poker room outlined around us. That meant, I was sure, that real world rules played. That Laverne and Stan were still with me in spirit.

I leaned forward. "Any of these men actually due to arrive in your world today?"

She glanced around at the frozen faces staring at her chest. "No."

"So then you're basically after me. Right?"

She said nothing, but I could tell from her eyes that I was right. I also knew without a doubt I wasn't ever destined to go in this direction after I died. Besides, from what I understood, superheroes lived a long time, so I had no idea how long in the future any question about this issue was going to be.

"Why go after a superhero?" I asked.

She smiled. "Challenge."

"It must be getting dull in Gambling Hell."

She only shrugged and smiled.

I had played her right into my hand and there was no point in rubbing salt into a wound any more, even if the person was from Gambling Hell and didn't know they were even wounded yet. So instead I smiled at her for a few moments longer, just to get her squirming.

Then I said, "Well, if you like a challenge, how about we finish this hand to see which direction this table is going? I win the hand we go up, back to the Mirage and you go somewhere else to play. You win, we go down, and I'll go with you for a while. Play your game."

The moment I put it back on the cards I caught a slight, very slight hint of panic cross her face. She hid it well, but I still saw it. I knew I had her. She had a good hand, but she didn't have the nut hand.

"Well, let us go so the dealer can call the hand," she said.

"No," I said, not wanting this table to get any closer to

that cavern floor. "Right here, right now. No more bets. We roll the cards and see who wins. Otherwise I call in Stan and he puts this table back where it belongs and you lose the chance of getting these players and me as your toys."

Heidi stared at me, taking her turn trying to read me. She was good, of that I had no doubt. But the best players in the world had tried to put reads on me for years without luck. No chance a simple Denizen from Gambling Hell could do it.

Finally she nodded. "You have a bet."

"I win," I said, making the bet clear, "the table goes back to the Mirage and you leave. You win, I release the table and we play in your world for a while."

"Those are the stakes," she said.

With that she flipped over pocket aces.

"Nice hand," I said.

And then I did something I never do in real life because it just annoys me and every other player. I hesitated in turning over my cards. It's called slow-rolling and it is the worst thing any player can do. But I did it anyway, just to get under Heidi's skin, just to give her a brief moment when she thought she had won. Sort of a little taste of her own hell is the way I figured it.

"Pocket kings," I said, flipping my cards onto the table face up in front of me. "Kings-full."

For a moment I thought I caught a glimpse of what Heidi really looked like under all that fake skin and large breasts. And let me tell you, she was one ugly human being. Nightmare ugly.

She stood, pushing her chair back and I let us go back to normal time at the same moment.

Suddenly the noise from the Mirage poker room pounded in around us. The men at the table were suddenly very surprised that Heidi was standing, and that our cards were showing without a final round of betting.

"Nice *playing* with you," she said, staring at me. Then without her false smile, she bent over and picked up her chips, giving a number of the men at the table a real show before turning and stamping off.

"What just happened there?" the dealer asked as he slid the pile of chips in the middle of the table toward me.

I shrugged. "Sore loser."

One of the men who had gotten the best show from her picking up her chips laughed. "She bends over like that a few more times and she can take all my money."

"Always be careful what you ask for," I said. "You never know where you might end up."

Everyone around the table laughed and the mood shifted back to fun game of serious poker, playing for money instead of souls.

The Match

CHAPTER ONE

I had a hunch that something was very, very wrong when I woke up in my own bed, in my doublewide trailer in the Oregon Coast Mountains. I know it sounds weird to say I knew something was wrong because I woke up in my own bed. Where else was I supposed to wake up, after all?

Problem being, I hadn't slept in that bed in years. Every night I normally slept with Patty Ledgerwood, aka Front Desk Girl, my girlfriend and sidekick. And she didn't much like (read that hated) my old doublewide, so we always stayed in her apartment in Las Vegas.

I didn't remember us having a fight.

And my sheets didn't smell musty from lack of use for years.

So something was very wrong.

Outside a slight rain and wind was rattling the windows and drumming on the flat roof.

In five or six months, Patty and I would have a big new mansion built on land I owned up in the mountains near here that we had designed together. But until that was finished, we stayed in her wonderful apartment in Las Vegas.

I remembered going to bed last night with her.

She had already been asleep, since I had gotten in late from a tournament at the Bellagio. I remember clearly she cuddled with me for a moment, still asleep, then rolled over.

As always, she had smelled wonderful and I remember rolling over as well, thinking I was the luckiest man alive.

Which, I had to admit, I was.

So how did I get here?

Was I sleep-teleporting or something?

I put on my clothes, which were Levis, tennis shoes, a plain dress shirt, black Fedora-like hat and black leather coat that was my uniform. I got my power from casinos, and it felt that when I had that coat and hat on I could channel the power better.

Then I jumped back to Patty's apartment.

Only I didn't jump.

I didn't go anywhere.

I just stood there in the middle of the doublewide's living room with a face that looked like I might take a crap on the green shag carpet at any moment.

Normally I just thought about where I wanted to go, concentrated, and then went there.

I tried again.

Nothing.

My old couch with a tan blanket covering it still sat there, a half-eaten tv dinner filled the center of the fake-wood coffee table, and the rain still drummed on the roof.

For some reason, my ability to teleport was shut off.

I felt a slight twisting of worry in my stomach, but there were a thousand reasons for this happening, not the least of which was a practical joke by one of the gods.

I did another quick check of the living room of my big doublewide to see if I could see anything at all different. The big box television was on as I normally left it on when here. Sort of background sounds.

I moved over into the kitchen area and checked my fridge. It was stocked, something I hadn't done in a couple years, and there were a few dirty dishes in the sink that didn't even look that crusty yet.

Whoever had done this to me had gotten the details right.

There was a carton of unopened milk in the fridge. I always kept milk there, and I went to open it for a drink to try to calm my twisting stomach. That was when I noticed the sell-by date.

June 18, 1999.

Only the milk inside was very fresh.

That date was almost a year before I was first approached by Stan to be a superhero.

I put the milk back without drinking any of it.

My stomach was now twisting a lot harder than it had a

moment before. Had something happened that shifted me back in time? I had learned that time travel was possible, but very protected by the gods and not allowed. In fact, from my understanding, there were very few gods who could even do it.

Had I been sleepwalking through time? Not likely. Which left only one conclusion.

Someone had sent me back here.

But who would send me back to this date and why?

Actually I didn't know the exact date.

I went over to the television and flipped around a few channels until I hit one with a running banner.

It said the day was June 7th, 1999. It was 10:07 in the morning Pacific Daylight Time.

I dropped onto the couch and tried to remember for a moment what I was doing on this day in 1999. All I knew that in general I was a professional poker player and winning my share. Even though I lived like a broke gambler in an old doublewide trailer with furnishings decades out of date, I was already pretty rich by the early summer of 1999.

Actually very, very rich.

And I was still years from meeting Patty.

But what I had done on June 7th, 1999 was beyond me.

Finally, I had had enough. I glanced up at the ceiling and shouted "Stan, a little help?"

I have no idea why I shouted at the ceiling for my boss, Stan, the God of Poker. But I always did.

He didn't appear.

"Hey, Stan, funny joke. Now tell me what's happening?"

No Stan.

And without Stan, that meant I had no team either to help me solve this.

I stood and headed for the front door. I needed to get to a casino and the closest one was my home casino, Spirit Winds, about a mile away.

I opened the door not knowing what to expect.

The old black Thunderbird that I had sold in 2010 was sitting out front in the gravel driveway where I always used to park. The doublewide was tucked in under some tall pine and the rain was dripping through the trees.

I took the keys off the hook beside the front door where I always left them and went out.

The Thunderbird started right up. I let it warm up a little and checked my wallet. I had just under five hundred, which was a pretty normal amount for me to carry at that point in time. Even my 1999 driver's license was current.

As I approached the big casino, I could see that the new additions had not yet been added.

I really was in 1999.

And totally alone once again.

Chapter Two

My stomach was twisting like a bad pretzel under a carnival vender's heat lamp. I was going to need some food and time to think. And some power from the casino.

I parked in my normal spot around to the side of the big building and headed inside, letting the power of the casino fill me. I flat loved walking into casinos. They felt like my home and I could always feel the power they gave me, even before I had become a superhero.

The casino power calmed me as I strode toward the buffet in its old location across from the front door.

Then suddenly it dawned on me that maybe the reason I couldn't teleport to Patty's apartment was because it wasn't there yet. It didn't get built until 2004 and her apartment was on the fourteenth floor.

Damn this time travel stuff could give a guy a headache.

I quickly turned and went into the men's restroom. No one was in there.

Then I thought of the front room of my trailer and jumped there.

It worked.

Worked fine, actually.

I clicked off the television I had left on when I left a few minutes earlier, feeling very, very relieved that I still had my powers.

I wasn't losing my mind completely.

I jumped back to the casino's men's room and resumed my journey to the buffet for breakfast. Somehow I needed to figure out why I was here, who had sent me here, and how to get back to 2014.

And without my team, I had no idea how to even start doing that.

What worried me even more was that someone had done this to get me out of the way. If I disappeared into the past, out of contact, my team might not be able to stop what danger might be happening in 2014.

I paid for breakfast and asked for a table against the wall. As the woman seated me and took my orange juice order, I glanced around at the few people eating in the buffet. I didn't know a one of them. Or at least I didn't remember any of them.

And none of them seemed to be giving me any strange looks.

I filled my plate with some ham, scrambled eggs, and a piece of toast and sat down with my back to the wall. No one said hello or even gave me a second glance.

I took myself out of time, freezing everyone around me. It felt like I stopped time, but I really didn't. I just stepped into a bubble between instants of time.

The sounds from the kitchen and the casino floor vanished, leaving me in complete silence.

The stepping between instants of time power was one of my most favorite powers. Right up there next to teleportation.

I took a bite of the eggs, then the ham, letting any of the gods who might be paying attention figure out there was a time bubble here that no one knew about. I knew these things were fairly easy to see for most gods.

After a full minute, I once again said, "Stan! Calling Stan, the God of Poker."

I imagined him clearly.

He appeared in front of me, frowning, not something I normally saw on my boss's face. The guy had the best poker face of anyone I had ever met. He was dressed as he always did, in tan slacks, a tan shirt, a plain button-down sweater and loafers. His short hair made him the plainest person I had ever met.

He glanced around at the time bubble, then back at me.

"How did you do this? And who are you?"

"My name is Poker Boy," I said. "And you recruit me out

of this casino to be a superhero in about a year. You taught me how to do this a few years later."

He opened his mouth and shut it.

"I somehow got pulled here from 2014. I have no idea how or why."

"Time travel is not allowed," he said.

"I know," I said. "You want to tell the person who did this to me?"

He opened his mouth, then shut it again without saying a word. I knew how he was feeling. Time travel was a scary thing and even my telling him as much as I had might change history. But I had to take that chance.

I indicated that he sit down and he did in the chair across from me.

"I am figuring that in the future someone needed me out of the way," I said. "So who, among the gods, could do this? Trap me back here? More than likely Laverne, but she wouldn't do this, so who else?"

He started to answer, but I stopped him. "I don't want to know. We need to be careful. I just need you and Laverne to figure this out and then tell me how I get back to 2014 without going through the last, or next, as the case might be, 15 years."

He nodded and vanished.

I moved myself back into the flow of time and the sounds came crashing back around me. Then I went to work on my breakfast again. When I got back to my own time, I'd ask Stan about this one. I had a hunch he was going to remember more about this day than I did at this moment.

I didn't want to think about where the real me was at this moment.

At least I hadn't woken up this morning next to myself. That might have been a tough thing to explain.

But my car had been in front of my trailer. So if I hadn't been home, exactly where was the other me?

Then I had the worst thought of the morning.

Maybe the old me had switched places with me in the future.

"Oh, I'm sorry, Patty," I said out loud, shaking my head and smiling at that idea.

"You should be," a voice said beside me.

Suddenly I was back out of time, the noise of the casino and buffet gone, and Stan was sitting across from me, smiling.

And Patty was sitting beside me, giving me her pretend angry look.

She kissed me before I had time to even say anything.

And let me say, after thinking I was alone, stuck in the past, that kiss felt wonderful, even better than normal, which was going some with kissing Patty.

Chapter Three

Stan cleared his throat. "Sorry to break this up," he said, "but I'll be back in about one minute and we have to be very careful this is not seen."

"The past you?" I asked.

Stan nodded.

"And you have the other me in a time bubble waiting somewhere for this to finish up?"

"Got it," Stan said.

"You were cute," Patty said, smiling at me.

"Am I going to need counseling after waking up with an older woman?" I asked her, smiling.

She whacked me and laughed. "You might."

I turned to Stan, my Stan from the future. "So what do I do?"

"I can't tell you a thing," Stan said. "At least not at this point. It has to play out. And it concerns this time."

"Isn't this part of it playing out?" I asked.

"All we can say at the moment," Stan said, shaking his head.

"Watch yourself there as well," I said. "This might be to get me out of the way."

"Good thinking," Stan said.

But I could tell he didn't give it a second thought. So this had nothing to do with a threat in 2014. It was completely about something here in 1999.

"See you in about fifteen years," Patty said, kissing me again.

"Be nice to the other me," I said.

She winked. "Oh, I will."

Then they were both gone and the time bubble was gone. The sounds of the buffet came crashing back in.

I sipped on the last of my orange juice, thinking about her last joke. I sure couldn't be jealous of my girlfriend spending time with me, even though it wasn't really me. At least not the me of now.

I was pretty sure, from my memory, which seemed oddly blank for this time period, I hadn't been allowed to remember what had happened.

A moment later another time bubble formed around me, plunging me back into silence and the young Stan appeared. Actually, he looked exactly like the Stan in fifteen years. I even think he was dressed in the same sweater and slacks.

"The other you is in your time in the future," Stan said, sitting down.

Around us everyone remained frozen, some in stride, others with a mouthful of food.

"I know," I said and he looked surprised, again losing his normal poker face.

He started to ask a question, but I waved him off.

"Only thing that could happen. I can't think of one reason I would be brought back in time."

"To play poker," Stan said.

Now it was my turn to be surprised. "Not something you could handle. You are as good as I am, if not better."

"I am told I am not," Stan said.

Again I was surprised.

"Laverne switched you out last night," Stan said. "The window was so tight for the transfer that she did not have time to warn you. She sends her apologies."

"Window?" I asked, getting more confused by the moment.

Stan nodded. "The entity who is setting this up needs to think you are not a superhero yet. When Laverne learned of what was to happen, she only had a few seconds to act."

"I'm to play this entity?" I'd done that a few times, the most memorable being an alien who looked like a snake. Actually, it was the same snake alien who messed up the Garden of Eden.

"No," Stan said. "You are to play another professional poker player."

Now I was getting very, very worried. And not about playing another professional poker player, but about the stakes. This was a lot of trouble to go through to set up a friendly game. And clearly Laverne was worried about it as well.

"So what kind of alien invasion is this going to stop if I win?"

Stan actually laughed. "Don't I wish?"

Now I was beyond worried.

"If I lose the world ends?" I asked.

Again Stan just laughed and shook his head. "Wow, you develop a wild ego, don't you? I hope your poker is as good as the ego."

"Better," I said. "So what am I playing for?"

"My job," Stan said.

I kind of opened and then closed my mouth.

"So you are actually playing for your job as well," Stan said, half laughing. "Since I hire you."

All I could do was sit there and think over all of the times my team and I rescued the entire planet. I really was playing for everything. The survival of the entire world. But Stan, this Stan, would have no way of knowing that.

And I didn't dare tell him.

No wonder Laverne had sent me back here.

"So Bernice, the God of Keno, is the entity that set this up?" I asked.

It was Stan's turn to open his mouth, then shut it. He nodded.

"And a lot of betting is going on among gods right now. Correct?"

Again Stan nodded.

"Bernice makes a run at me a few years after you hire me to get your job that way. She tried using all her 'charms' on me and failed."

"Wow, you turned down those looks?" Stan said.

Model looks, a soft voice, and huge breasts didn't much do it for me. And her laugh sounded more like a baying donkey anyway. She was the best-looking of all the gods in classical beauty, and I didn't blame her for wanting to get out of the dead-end world of Keno. Only problem was, she had the brains of a Keno player.

As poker players like to joke, a Keno player is a gambler who has lost the will to live.

Why she kept making runs at Stan's job was beyond me. But if she got it this time, she would never hire me and the world would end at any number of different points in the next fifteen years when me and my team were not together to save it.

I was going to have to win this.

One way or another.

Chapter Four

"So I have to pretend I have no powers and don't understand what is happening? Right?"

Stan nodded.

"And no one has seen this time bubble?"

"Laverne's been blocking this," he said. "She feels it's critical that you win this."

Now I was puzzled again. "Isn't she the boss? Can't she just kill this entire idea?"

"I could," Laverne said, appearing next to the table in the time bubble. In the future, Laverne, known as Lady Luck, was always in my floating office over Las Vegas and was treated like one of the gang.

She had on her standard black business suit and her dark hair was pulled back, making her face seem all business.

1999 Stan scooted back and stood. He clearly didn't

spend much, if any, time around one of the most powerful gods and his boss at this point in time.

Laverne dropped into a chair and faced me. "If I have to, I'll pull rank on this. But it will damage my power base at this point in time."

"Bernice has been sleeping with a number of gods who would like a little more power, huh?" I asked.

"She may be as dumb as this fork," Laverne said, nodding, "but she can manipulate men. And she's dangerous."

"Does she have any idea what she's risking with this?" I asked.

Laverne glanced at the stunned look on Stan's face, then shook her head. "No, she would have no way of knowing. No one at her level in this time period would know. Just win this match."

"Can I use my powers?"

"Just the ones you had at this point in time," Laverne said. "Safer. A lot of gods will be watching."

I nodded. "I'll win it. But you already know that."

"Honestly, I don't," she said. "This entire thing is a side timeline on the normal timeline and I'm working to figure out who's doing this. And how and why. This did not originally happen in 1999 to you."

"No wonder I have no memory of any of this."

She nodded and said nothing.

"I'll still win it," I said, doing my best to keep my stomach from twisting right out of my side with sudden fear.

"Thanks," she said, and vanished.

I took a deep breath and glanced at the shocked look on Stan's face.

"So where and when?"

"You need to get to Vegas in two days," he said. "Special room set up at Binion's Horseshoe."

"Who am I playing?" I asked.

"Doc Hill," he said.

And my stomach twisted one more twist tighter which, up until that point, I didn't think it could. Doc Hill was the best No Limit Hold'em player in the world. Even in 2014 I didn't often play against him, since he was mostly a tournament player. But in 1999 he was coming off of two years as *Card Player Magazine* Player of the Year and he had won more World Series of Poker bracelets than any person alive.

My future just looked a lot dimmer. And my promise to Lady Luck sounded like bluster instead of fact. Doc Hill was going to be damn hard to beat.

I hoped Lady Luck and my team in the future could figure who was doing this and why before I had to sit down across from Doc.

CHAPTER FIVE

I hadn't been on an airline since I had learned how to teleport. And after the two hours in the airport and the four-hour flight to Vegas, I didn't miss airports and the lines and the waiting. Not in the slightest. And I swore they had put the seats closer together. Even in first class.

I took a cab to Binion's Horseshoe Casino and Hotel in the downtown area. At this point in time, Fremont Street had not been covered with the light show and the area had a feel of being rundown.

Binion's hadn't seemed to change. There were low ceilings and far too much smoke in the air. I felt the power from the casino fill me as I walked in, but then a moment later I coughed. My lungs were just not used to all the smoke. It was amazing how much that one detail had changed in fifteen years.

I headed through the clouds of smoke and past the small poker area toward the hotel front desk.

And there, standing behind the desk, was my future girlfriend, Patty Ledgerwood.

I damn near fell flat on my face. In 2002, after I had been a superhero for a number of years, I would come here for the last time the World Series of Poker was held in this casino. And I would meet Patty at the front desk, just like this.

And she would become my sidekick and my girlfriend.

She was dressed in the Binion's Hotel uniform of the time. Brown dress slacks, a white blouse, and a light brown vest with a nametag on the vest.

Somehow, I was going to have to talk with her. I was going to have to be very, very careful.

And not trip over the ropes that blocked off the front like I did the first time I met her.

As I approached the desk, she looked up and winked at me. "Enjoy the flight?"

I was stunned. I leaned in over the counter and whispered, "Patty?"

She smiled and I knew it was my Patty from the future. "Laverne has the entire team back here," she whispered, "trying to figure out who's doing this."

Then she said in a normal voice, "Would you like to check in, sir?"

"I would," I said, and gave her my real-world name.

"Flying sucks," I whispered and she laughed that wonderful high laugh of hers as she checked her computer.

"We have you in a suite," she said, sliding me the paper-work I needed to sign. "Laverne has it blocked," she whispered, "so we'll all see you there later with an update."

"Wonderful," I said in my normal voice.

She handed me my key card and I took it. "Thanks for the great service."

"Oh, that comes later," she whispered without moving her lips.

It was everything I could do to not laugh and not trip over the ropes on the way out of the front desk area.

I couldn't begin to say how relieved I was that the team was here.

And how much I was in love with that girl behind the front desk.

CHAPTER SIX

Patty, Stan, Screamer, and Ben all appeared in my suite about an hour after I had settled into the place. You could tell the suite had seen better days, but I knew that in a few years the entire hotel would be remodeled and would turn out wonderful.

Patty was still in her Binion's uniform, Stan looked the same in both timelines, Screamer had on his standard jeans, sweater, and tennis shoes, and Ben was dressed like an old librarian, only without the tie.

It felt fantastic to see them again. Not only were we all a team, but they were my closest friends.

On the long flight down, I had come up with a few conclusions and I wanted to run them past the team. I had no idea where the Stan of this time was. Or where any of the 1999 members of the team were. Not sure I wanted to know.

Patty hugged me, then kissed me, then we all gathered in the suite's living room area.

I looked at Ben, who was the oldest member of the team and was now a god in the book and reading area. He had a memory of every fact about the gods known or not known.

"Who is the God of Time?" I asked Ben as we settled in.

"Chronos," Ben said.

I nodded. I sort of had known that.

"Does he have a younger son he's training?"

"He does," Ben said, nodding, but looking puzzled. "Two of them, actually."

"You don't think Tick or Tock have anything to do with this?" Stan asked, his face very serious.

"Tick? Tock?" I asked, trying my best not to laugh. Never a good idea to laugh at the gods. "Nicknames I hope?"

I glanced around, but not one of my team seemed to think those names odd or funny in any way.

"No," Ben said, also very serious.

I took a deep breath to calm myself to keep from laughing, then asked the next question. "Which one has an outsized interest in women? Or reputation as a woman chaser?"

"Tock," Stan said. "It's gotten him in trouble more than once over the centuries. But I don't see why you think he might have something to do with this. It was Laverne that brought you back from the future."

"I know," I said, nodding. "But how did any of the gods of this time even know who I was?"

Stan started to open his mouth to answer, then shut it.

"You don't recruit me for almost a year," I said. "At this point in time I'm just a good local grinder. So only someone with the ability to see through time would know about me," I said.

"But Doc Hill could beat just about anyone of this time," Patty said. "If Bernice is behind this, why pick a player that might actually have a shot at beating Doc?"

"Because she and her boyfriend don't really know me," I said. "But his dad would be able to see the problem if Bernice became the God of Poker."

"And he would pick the player," Stan said.

"And give Laverne enough time to switch me out," I said, nodding. "And put this entire thing off in a side loop in time without anyone knowing."

"You being here is finally starting to make sense," Stan said and everyone was nodding.

"Only one more question," I said, "that I can't figure out."

Everyone looked at me, waiting.

"Why did Doc Hill agree to this match?"

Silence from my team.

"He wouldn't," I said. "He's richer than I am and that's going some, so money isn't a factor. And I'm an unknown at this point in time, so there's no fun in playing an unknown player heads-up. He would never agree unless..."

"Tock and Bernice are holding something over him," Screamer said.

I nodded. "I know this much about Doc Hill. At this

point in time, he doesn't care about his father. But he and his mother and his grandfather are very close. And his best friend is his lawyer. Any of them in danger would force him to agree to this."

"I wonder if Tock's father knows about this?"

"I doubt it," I said.

Stan nodded and looked at me. "Well, he's going to. Stay put. The match is scheduled to start on the second floor in three hours. We have work to do."

They were suddenly all gone.

I looked around. Since Stan didn't want me leaving, that meant I couldn't go to the great steak restaurant on the upper floor. But I could go for room service.

If I ended up having to play Doc Hill, I wanted to at least go into it on a full stomach.

Chapter Seven

I had just finished with my steak and fries and was sitting back watching 1999 news, which seemed both fresh and strange at the same time, when Stan, Patty, Laverne, and Doc Hill appeared in my room.

They were all smiling, except Doc, who just looked stunned.

"All wrapped up?" I asked as I clicked off the television.

Laverne nodded.

I was surprised that they had brought Doc. More than likely his memory would be erased. He had no powers and no real reason to know about any of this sort of thing.

He was looking around, clearly having troubles getting grounded. He was a tall man and clearly young. If I remembered right, he had only left college a few years ago just short of a doctorate in something, which is why they called him Doc. He had long, sun-streaked brown hair and a deep tan. He rafted summers in the Idaho wilderness and seemed to be naturally good at anything he did.

"I am pretty sure I don't want to know how you did that," Doc said, looking around at the room before looking at Stan.

Stan nodded. "You don't."

"Great seeing you again, Doc," I said, moving to shake his hand, then realized he looked even more confused. "Great meeting you, at least."

"And who are you?" Doc asked.

"I'll become known as Poker Boy," I said. "I was the one you were supposed to play. Have you met the others?"

He shook his head. "Patty Ledgerwood," I said, introducing Patty. When she shook his hand I could see him visibly calm down. I loved that power of hers to do that.

I pointed to Stan. "He's the God of Poker and that's Laverne, Lady Luck herself."

He started to say something, then stopped. "If I hadn't just been teleported here, I would be laughing."

"Don't blame you," I said.

I glanced at Laverne. "I assume he's not going to remember any of this?"

"This side timeline will vanish when we return," Laverne said. "And Doc, we would like to apologize for the worry. Your mother will be fine and not remember any of this either."

"And that's why I had no memory of it," I said.

"We'll remember it now," Stan said. "It happened in our timeline in 2014."

"Now that makes sense," I said. "But why bring Doc here?"

"We have a lot of the gods interested in this match between you two," Laverne said.

I laughed. "Of course they are. But no nasty problems over the outcome?"

"Nothing," Laverne said. "But there are a lot of bets among gods."

"Which way are the odds?" I asked.

Laverne laughed. "Since they have discovered it's actually you, Poker Boy, playing the match, the odds have tightened up. They are now two-to-one."

"That I win?" I asked.

Laverne shook her head. "That Doc kicks your ass."

Now it was my turn to feel stunned and Patty and Stan both laughed. Even Doc smiled.

I looked at him. "You up for a match?'

He smiled and shrugged. "Why not? No limit hold'em, heads-up, best of five matches. No superpowers or whatever you have."

"No powers beyond normal poker player powers," I said.

He nodded and I shook his hand, agreeing to the match. "You ready?"

"Any time," he said.

Laverne smiled and jumped us to a private room on the second floor of Binion's Horseshoe Casino.

I was in heaven. I got to play the best poker player in the world heads-up. It didn't get any better than this, even if I had to travel back in time 15 years to do it.

Now the key was to not make a fool of myself.

CHAPTER EIGHT

The room we were in had high ceilings and was mostly used by the casino as a banquet room I was sure, with the red felt wallpaper of old casinos and polished wood pillars. The poker table we were to play at was square in the middle of the room under a bright light. On three sides were grandstands ten seats high, making the table feel like it was in the bottom of a pit.

A male dealer with a Binion's uniform sat at the table, the cards spread out in front of him as was standard. There were no chips in his tray, but two stacks of chips were in positions facing each other down the length of the table.

Patty kissed me for luck, then she and Stan and Lady Luck moved over to the stands and sat down near the middle. The rest of the stands were empty at the moment.

"So that really is Lady Luck?" Doc asked, standing there beside me next to the table, clearly trying to get his footing.

I was amazed he wasn't just sitting in a chair with his head in his hands. Clearly the guy was as good as dealing with pressure and unusual circumstances as people said he was. It didn't come any more unusual than this.

"It is," I said.

"Is she going to help you then?"

I laughed. "Even if she could, she wouldn't. Luck is a natural force in the world. She's the god of that force. She'll just let it run its natural course and make sure, at the same time, no one else interferes."

Doc nodded. Then he turned to face me. "How about a side bet?"

I looked at him and shook my head. "Lady Luck won't let you remember any of this."

He waved his hand. "Trust me, I don't want to."

"So what kind of bet are you thinking of."

He looked at me with those intense brown eyes and suntanned face. "You look a little pale. I assume I'm still running the rivers in Idaho in 2014."

"You are," I said.

"If I win," Doc said, "since you'll remember this, you and your girlfriend book a raft trip with me."

Even though I hated the very idea, I had to act brave. I motioned for Patty to come over and told her the idea.

She just laughed and said she would make sure I held up

my end of the deal if I lost. She would love to go on a raft trip into the Idaho Primitive Area.

I, on the other hand, was more scared of that idea than facing the alien snake that had screwed up the Garden of Eden.

"And if I win," I asked.

Doc Hill just smiled. "You'll always know you beat the best tournament player in the world at his own game."

Patty laughed. "And I thought Poker Boy had an ego when it came to cards. Does that come with being a poker player?"

Both Doc and I said at the same time, "It does."

Chapter Nine

ROUND ONE:

The rules were pretty simple in heads-up No-Limit Hold'em. We both started with the same amount of chips, in this case $500,000. The chips were in denominations of one thousand, five thousand, and twenty-five thousand.

When one person had the full million and the other player had no chips, the round was over.

Winner of the best of five rounds won the match.

The blinds were one thousand for the small blind and two thousand for the large blind.

In Hold'em, there was a dealer's button, which was the position that always got to bet last after the first round. In heads-up, the dealer button was under the small blind and before the flop (first three cards) the small blind had to act first.

After the flop the other player had to act first.

Position from that button was critical in all Hold'em poker, even more so in heads-up play.

So I shook Doc's hand, tried to clear out the idea of going into the Idaho Primitive area, and we sat down facing each other.

Again, the young poker player in me came screaming back in, all happy and excited. I was actually facing the best poker player on the planet in a private match. It didn't get any better than this.

Doc drew the button first and I tossed out my big blind of two thousand and he put a one thousand dollar chip on top of the button. A half million might seem like a lot of money, but in this game it wouldn't last long.

The dealer, a middle-aged man who clearly worked for the gods somewhere, shuffled the cards, tapped the table and asked, "Ready, gentleman?"

We both said we were

As he shuffled, the grandstands around us filled.

I saw some gods I knew and a few hundred I didn't. An older guy with a long white beard was now sitting next to Laverne. I guessed that was Chronos.

On the other side of him was a younger guy I assumed was his son, Tock. Beside him was Bernice, dressed to kill and with larger breasts than I remembered. But she had a very sour look on her classically-beautiful face and kept brushing Tock's hand off her leg.

That was going to be a very short-lived relationship.

I looked at Doc, who had his mouth open and was just staring.

"Better to not ask and just forget," I said.

He swallowed hard and looked back at me, nodding.

He had to call the bet first. He glanced at his two cards and folded.

We exchanged blinds for the next few hands and I could sense that Doc Hill was slowly starting to get his feet under him.

On his third big blind I raised him and he folded.

He called with his next small blind, I raised him, and he folded again.

I wasn't even really looking at my cards. I just needed to build up a little cushion while he was off balance. But I had no doubt that advantage wouldn't last long.

I took two more of his hands before he finally decided to fight back with a medium-sized raise of twenty-five thousand.

I happened to have two eights in my hand, a fantastic hand in heads-up, so I re-raised him four times his bet, shoving out one-hundred thousand.

He cold called.

The flop showed another eight. Plus an ace and a deuce, all colors.

I checked my set, hoping to trap him. What I really hoped was that he had an ace in his hand.

He bet one-hundred thousand.

I raised, pushing my entire stack in.

He had no choice, since I assumed he had hit his ace. He would be crippled if he lost that hand.

He shook his head, knowing what happened as he called. My three eights stood up against his pair of aces.

First round to me.

And around us the gods applauded.

CHAPTER TEN

ROUND TWO:

As I had been afraid would happen, Doc Hill finally got his feet under him and ignored the strange people sitting all around us.

He came after me at the start of the second round like a mother trying to protect her child and I was the attacker.

He raised every hand to ten thousand. That was a small raise, but still effective at chewing up a stack of chips.

My chips.

And when I raised him on the third hand, he just re-raised back, forcing me to fold like a bad cliché about wet paper.

I flat called two of his raises in the first ten hands and had to fold into his betting pressure because the flop had missed my cards entirely.

In No-Limit Hold'em, aggressive action tended to win

more than it lost. I could be aggressive with the best of them, but after those first ten hands of Round Two, I felt I had been pushed through a buzz saw and cut down to size. He handled me like I handled a low-level player.

And I hated that feeling.

Once the momentum of aggression was set, it was damn hard to shut it off. I knew that from experience.

I had about three hundred thousand left, not in panic mode, but close.

So I folded to his raises three more hands, then suddenly re-raised him one hundred thousand, letting him think I had a decent hand for the first time. I actually had a jack-nine off-suit. Not horrible, but not bad for this kind of game.

He didn't even blink. He re-raised me by shoving all in.

If I folded, my two-hundred thousand against his eight-hundred thousand would be like throwing chum in a tank full of sharks. He would chew it up in a matter of minutes.

My best bet right now was to ride the hand with my jack-nine. If it won, I was back in the round.

I called and he flipped over queen-six off-suit.

His hand was slightly better statistically.

But not by that much.

And then on the flop he hit his second queen and Round Two went to him with the Gods again applauding.

CHAPTER ELEVEN

ROUND THREE: Doc came out aggressive again in the third round and this time I fired right back, matching aggressive move with aggressive move.

On the fourth hand I finally got him to lay a hand down with a two-hundred thousand raise.

As the dealer shuffled, Doc smiled at me and nodded. "Tough to stop a steamroller, isn't it? Well done."

"And to you as well," I said. "And thanks again for doing this."

"Are you kidding?" he asked. "Getting to play against a player at your level is something I don't get to do very often."

"This is fun, isn't it?" I asked as the dealer dealt out our cards.

"As fun as having you and Patty in whitewater rapids with me."

He smiled at me.

I shuddered.

From the nearby stands I heard Patty laugh.

And then Doc raised before I had time to even get my mind out of the terror of an Idaho Wilderness trip.

Four hands later, we were still about even in chips. Doc glanced at his cards and flat called my big blind.

I looked down at my two hole cards. I had an Ace-King of hearts, nicknamed "A Big Slick." That was one of the most powerful hands in all of poker, especially heads-up. It wasn't a made hand, but it was powerful.

So hoping to get Doc betting and trap him, I just checked and we went to the flop.

The flop came ace, ten, four. The four was a heart.

I had a pair of aces. In heads-up it didn't come any more powerful.

Doc would expect me to bet into that flop since we were playing aggressive poker, so I did, making the bet fifty thousand. I wanted him to think I was over-betting it to take the blinds.

He thought for a moment and called.

I had no idea why he called. Maybe he had a small pair, maybe he just figured I had nothing.

Or maybe he had an ace as well.

The next card came a six of hearts.

I checked. My check forced him into betting to get me out of the pot. He bet a smooth one-hundred thousand.

I called and he looked up at me, trying to get a read on me.

I could read nothing from him.

Nothing.

The next card came ten of hearts. So I had the best flush possible.

I bet out exactly the size of his last bet. One-hundred thousand.

He pushed all in.

I called.

He rolled over a pair of aces for aces full over tens.

I didn't show him my flush.

Round three to Doc.

The audience of Gods applauded.

I was down two rounds to one against the best poker player on the planet. This was not looking good for me staying off a raft in the middle of a river.

Chapter Twelve

ROUND FOUR: For almost a half hour, Doc and I exchanged raises and folds at the start of the new round, ending up pretty close to where we started.

That's a very long time for no one to make a move in no-limit heads-up poker.

I just couldn't find a weakness anywhere in his game. And he seemed to be in my head more than I was in his.

The way he trapped me with those aces in the last round was masterful. So while I thought I was trapping him, he had me already at a huge disadvantage.

So after thirty minutes, I figured that the best way to play him in this fourth round was just to do what he did to me in the second round.

I just stared raising everything, and re-raising him on his raises.

I could see he knew what I was doing and was just waiting to be dealt some decent cards to make me pay.

If I had a chance at all, I needed to get him doubting he had a read on me.

So as my chips passed six hundred thousand, he raised. If I followed my pattern, I would re-raise him.

Instead I just tossed the cards in the muck.

He looked up at me, surprised.

He had a hand and was about to teach me a lesson. My folding gave him pause.

He leaned forward slightly as the dealer shuffled. "Bring a suit for swimming in the river and a heavy coat for the nights around the campfire."

He sat back, smiling at me.

Again I heard Patty laugh.

There were a lot of weapons in poker and Doc Hill was showing me how to blatantly use them all. Time for me to play that same game a little.

"I will," I said, smiling back. "I'm just glad we're not playing to save the entire world as we were planning to do."

He tried to keep the smile on his face.

Again the wonderful laugh of my girlfriend got to my ears.

After a moment Doc glanced at the audience, then back at his cards.

I raised and he folded, muttering something about "Well-played."

I went back to being aggressive, slowly chipping away at his chips.

Then he cold-called one of my raises.

I had king-ten off-suit. The flop missed me completely.

I raised fifty thousand.

He again flat called like a beginner would do against a raise.

The turn card missed me as well.

I checked.

He checked.

Again a beginner play. But I knew for a fact I didn't have him that rattled.

The river card also missed my two cards. I had King high.

I checked.

He checked.

I rolled over my king.

He rolled over an ace and took the pot.

And suddenly we were back to almost even.

Doc Hill turned back into a buzz saw, raising and re-raising everything.

I had to fold just about everything for six hands as he took the chip lead.

Then as he raised, I glanced down and saw a pair of tens. Great hand in heads-up.

I re-raised him with one hundred thousand.

He re-raised me all in.

I called.

He had more chips than I did, so my entire tournament life was on the line.

I rolled over my tens.

Doc nodded and rolled over ace-jack.

This was called "A Race" because the statistical odds were pretty even going into the flop, especially when you take into account the straight possibilities.

Everyone in the audience knew it might be over and they were all standing.

Doc stayed seated.

I stayed seated.

There was an ace on the flop.

The odds of my surviving went to very small. I could only win if one of the other two tens came out of the deck.

They did not.

I lost the fourth round.

And the match.

All the Gods applauded and then vanished as I stood to shake Doc's hand.

The entire thing had taken just under two hours.

And even though I had lost, I had enjoyed those two hours more than I wanted to admit.

"That was great fun," Doc said, shaking my hand.

"It really was," I said. "Thanks for taking part."

"My pleasure," Doc said, "even though I'm not going to remember it. See you on the river in about fifteen years."

"We'll be there," Patty said, coming over and taking my arm.

With that Doc vanished.

Right behind him the room faded.

And then 1999 vanished.

Chapter Thirteen

I woke up in 2014 next to Patty in her apartment. She rolled over against me and sighed, still mostly asleep. She smelled wonderful, like soft roses and faint earth.

Around the edges of the sun-blocking drapes, the Las Vegas day looked bright and dry, not at all like the rain in Oregon.

That had been one very strange dream.

I lay there on my back, holding the love of my life, staring at the ceiling, thinking back over the dream of going back to 1999 and playing Doc Hill.

It had felt so real.

It had to have been real. But yet I remember clearly coming home late last night from the Bellagio tournament and crawling in with Patty.

After a moment, Patty stirred, and opened one eye. When

she saw I was awake, she laughed softly. "Stewing about Doc beating you?"

So it hadn't been a dream.

Then I remembered Laverne had said it had been a loop in the normal timeline, so of course we had returned to the moment the loop started to end it.

"Not stewing," I said, hugging her. "I gave him a good fight."

"It was a lot of fun to watch," she said, snuggling against me and closing her eyes. "You did better than Doc expected. You even won the first of the four matches, remember?"

"Before he got a read on me," I said. "Thank heavens there was no life on the line."

"Or world destruction," Patty said.

"Yeah, that too," I said.

"Just a wonderful trip into the Idaho Wilderness."

I tried not to shudder. The Oregon Mountains where my doublewide trailer was were wild enough for me.

She leaned up on one elbow and looked me right in the eyes. "Is he that good or did you let him win?"

I laughed. "He's that good. And no real poker player ever lets another win for any reason."

She smiled and kissed me. "You're still my superhero."

I kissed her back and pressed against her. After a moment we came up for air and she looked at me again, her wonderful brown eyes twinkling. "We might have to change your super-hero name, though."

"To what?" I asked, holding her fantastic body tight against me.

"Well, it sure can't be "River Man," she said.

I laughed.

"I'm thinking right now," she said, "about something like "Man of Steel.""

She kissed me and I kissed her back, doing my best to live up to my new superhero name.

Dried Up

CHAPTER ONE

I very seldom get the feeling that something is wrong while sleeping beside Patty Ledgerwood, aka Front Desk Girl. In fact, until that very moment, it had never happened. Nothing ever seemed to be wrong when I was with Patty and not on a mission.

I get the "something-is-wrong" feeling at poker tables all the time, usually when another professional player is attempting to bluff me out of my shoes and all my money. I have learned to pay attention to that feeling, almost as if it is one of my superpowers. By paying attention, I have saved myself a ton of money over the years.

Right now I was in Patty's apartment near the University of Nevada, Las Vegas campus. In her master bedroom, to be exact. I could hear her regular breathing beside me, which told me she was sound asleep. The wonderful smell of her rose perfume filled the air and the feel of her expensive, fine-cotton sheets against my mostly bare skin felt wonderful, just as they always did.

Patty had had the day off, and we had spent it together; first at a movie, then a nice dinner at the buffet at the MGM Grand, and then back to her apartment to cuddle on the couch and watch television before heading to bed.

It didn't get much better these days.

But now, even without opening my eyes, I knew something was wrong.

I eased one eye open without moving, and couldn't see a thing in the dark room. The only light came from a nightlight in the bathroom to the right of the room and an alarm clock on the nightstand beside me. There was no light coming under the heavy curtains over the patio door, so it was still dark outside as well.

I eased over to glance at the time, and a lightning storm went off in the sheets.

And that wasn't a metaphor for some sexual thing.

A real lightning storm erupted around me, as more static electricity than I could imagine let lose.

And each spark was like a kid pinching me. Let me tell you, the sparks hurt.

"Wow!" I said out loud as I sat up.

It was as if I had rubbed my entire body across a carpet and then was touching things.

My movement caused the sheets to explode with even more static electricity which woke Patty up, and she sat bolt upright in bed as well, causing even *more* sparks as she sat stunned at the light show going on around us.

And the tiny pinches of pain with every large spark.

Somehow, every bit of moisture had been sucked out of the room, and a very large, background, static electric charge had filled the air.

"Sit still," I said, as Patty moved slightly and the room lit up with a light show once again.

"Ouch!" Patty said, freezing in place. "That hurts."

I had heard of many reasons for friction in bed, but this was ridiculous.

But in the light caused by the sparks with Patty's last movement, I had seen the problem.

Two alien-looking creatures with large black eyes and oblong heads stood at the end of the bed, staring at us.

It was like a scene out of a bad alien-abduction movie.

The UFO conspiracy people called them "Grays," but I knew them to be members of a race native to Earth called the Silicon Suckers.

In fact, they had been around far, far longer than humans.

They hate water and could deal with very little if any of it. Clearly they took what water they needed right out of the air around them.

They lived in very dry caves in the desert. The caves were so dry, the air would kill a human after just a couple of days, even with enough drinking water, which wasn't allowed in the homes of the Silicon Suckers.

Their very presence in Patty's apartment had sucked all the moisture out of the room.

I had never heard of a Silicon Sucker being seen inside a human city. Something had to be very, very wrong.

I carefully motioned for Patty to look at the foot of the bed. The sparks from my slight movement bit into me again and lit up the room.

She saw them and her breath sucked in with surprise. She instinctively pulled the sheet up to her neck covering up her nightgown and causing a large electrical storm around her and me.

Damn those little sparks hurt. It was lucky we just didn't burst into flames right there.

"Sorry," she said, holding her breath against the pain.

I had dealt with the Silicon Suckers a number of times before, and been in their sacred caves they called "sand castles." I had always been welcomed in their world because of a couple of favors I had done for them over the last few years.

"Greetings, honored guests," I said, bowing my head slightly and hoping the movement wouldn't set the sheets on fire. "What do I owe this great honor?"

Both Silicon Suckers bowed in return. Both looked identical. The one on the right spoke.

"Poker Boy, Front Desk Girl, we ask for your assistance in a matter of importance to our people."

"Of course," I said.

Both Patty and I bowed slightly.

After the sparks stopped I said, "It will be a great honor to help our friends."

Both again bowed in acceptance. "Our leader will speak to you at sunrise."

"We will attend," I said, also bowing again and setting off even more sparks. This room was going to need a humidifier real quick or we would be calling for fire trucks.

Without another word, the two turned and went out through curtains covering the bedroom's patio door, setting off a huge wave of sparks. I knew for a fact that the door had been locked and secured when we had gone to bed.

I had no idea how they had gotten in, or how they would get from Patty's apartment near UNLV, across town, actually across the Strip, and back into the desert.

The moment the curtains dropped back into place in a shower of static electricity, I instantly transported us into the living room area of Patty's apartment. The air there felt dry, but nothing like the intense lack of moisture in the bedroom.

I loved my newly learned superpower of teleportation. I just never expected to use it teleporting out of Patty's bed.

Patty used a napkin to flip on a light, took one look at me and started to laugh.

Now trust me, a beautiful woman in a sheer blue nightgown laughing when she sees your almost-naked body does not do wonders for even my superhero ego.

But I had to admit she looked just as funny. Besides all the tiny red marks all over her arms and wonderful legs that showed under her nightgown, her long brown hair stuck out in all directions from her head like she had been attacked by a mad hairdresser. Her hair was spread so wide, I doubt she could even get through a door.

And her wonderful face looked like it had a bad case of measles.

I glanced down at my own legs and chest, also covered with hundreds and hundreds of small red marks, as if I had been attacked by a swarm of bed bugs. Then I felt my brown hair, which was also standing straight out in all directions. And I could also feel my face was covered in the tiny red bumps from the electrical shocks.

Thank heavens I had worn my boxers to bed. The thought of electronic shocks to certain parts of my body just made me shudder.

CHAPTER TWO

After we carefully opened the windows and doors to let in some of what now seemed like balmy and humid Las Vegas summer air, we both drank three large glasses of water.

Thirsty didn't begin to describe what I was feeling.

Then, when we both had extra-large glasses of water in our hands, I shouted at the ceiling. "Stan. Need help!"

I have no idea how he always heard me, but he always did. Stan was the God of Poker, and my immediate boss.

An instant later he appeared in Patty's living room in front of us, looking grumpy that I had disturbed him in the middle of the night. He normally wore brown slacks, a light sweater, and black shoes. He was a short man, not even close to my six-foot height, and I seldom saw him smile. His dark hair was cut very short all the time, and his eyes looked almost black.

But tonight he had on a white golf shirt and blue golf shorts and the shorts looked like they were on backwards. When the God of Poker can't even dress himself, he really was tired.

He started to say something, then took one look at us and started laughing. I had seen him laugh a few times, but when a God starts to laugh at you, it is always worrisome.

But I had to admit that we did look funny. There was no containing our hair and the red marks on our faces, arms, and legs were getting brighter by the second.

"You two go through a swarm of bees on a rollercoaster?"

"Nope," I said as he laughed. "Just an electrical storm in bed."

He started to make some joke, then looked at Patty, then back at me and couldn't say anything because he was laughing too hard.

"I'm not kidding," I said. "Two Silicon Suckers woke us up and asked for our help."

Stan's laughing instantly vanished and he went back to his normal poker face. His golf shirt and golf shorts instantly became his normal slacks and sweater and black shoes.

It seemed I now had his attention and he was very much awake.

"How in the world did they get here?" he asked, shaking his head. "And when are you supposed to meet them?"

"We are meeting their leader at sunrise."

"You are meeting the Great One?"

Now he was stunned and when he said it like that, it bothered me as well. Patty just looked worried under all the red marks and massive head of hair spread out three feet around her head. It was going to take her some real time once the static charge faded to untangle all that wonderful long hair.

"You ever heard of the Silicon Suckers coming into any human town?" I asked Stan. "Just to ask for human help?"

"Never," he said, shaking his head.

"Have you heard any rumors about anything going wrong in their caves? Or anyone having a run-in with them?"

"Nothing," he said, "but I might have missed something. Stay put, I'm going to go get Burt and maybe Laverne."

He vanished.

Laverne was Lady Luck herself, in charge of all of the gambling and gaming universe. Burt was her second in command. I'd been around Lady Luck a number of times now, and Patty and I and the team had actually saved her life once. But she still scared hell out of me.

If Stan thought this was worth waking up Burt and maybe even Laverne, then Patty and I really might be in over our heads. We were just lowly superheroes.

Really dry and marked-up superheroes.

I had just taken another drink of water and was about to suggest we get a little more dressed when Laverne and Stan appeared. Lady Luck had on a strict brown business suit with her brown hair pulled back tight in a bun. She did not look happy.

When she saw us she raised one eyebrow, but did not smile, even though we looked really, really silly. With a wave of her hand Patty and I were both dressed, the static gone from our hair and the red marks gone from our skin.

Patty in her normal black pants and white blouse. Laverne had put me in my normal jeans with dress shirt, black leather coat and Fedora-like black hat. That was my poker uniform.

"Thank you," Patty said.

I nodded agreement. "Yes, thank you. I feel much better."

I could also feel the extra power that my coat and hat brought to me from the nearby casinos.

"No idea at all what the Silicon Suckers want?" Lady Luck asked, all business.

"Not a clue," I said. "Has something like this ever happened before?"

"Never," she said. "I have only met The Great One once, a few thousand years ago. But I do know that he only concerns himself with matters of major importance."

"I wonder why he came to us instead of you?" Patty asked. "It makes no sense."

"He didn't want to bother you," I said to Lady Luck, knowing the answer to Patty's question. "This is something he feels Patty and I can accomplish."

Both Laverne and Stan nodded.

"That makes sense," Laverne said. "But it gets us no closer to what he might want. And we just don't have time to figure it out. You had better get going."

"We have one stop to make first," I said.

I turned to my direct boss. "Stan, could you get me six thermoses and two backpacks to carry them in, and meet me at The Diner?"

Stan nodded and vanished.

"Good luck," Laverne said. "If you need my help in any fashion, just call out. I will be standing by."

"Thank you," Patty said as Laverne vanished.

I glanced at Patty, who looked stunning, as always, in the dark slacks and white blouse that Laverne had dressed her in. Her brown hair was combed and under control. Only the worry showing in her dark-brown eyes flawed the picture.

"Ready for an adventure?" I asked.

"With you, always," she said, smiling.

I took her hand and jumped us to The Diner, our favorite restaurant and meeting place tucked off on a side street in downtown Las Vegas. It was a place decorated in a fake 1960s look and run by Madge, a superhero in the food service part of the world. Madge seemed to always be there and she made the best milkshakes on the planet.

Ten minutes later, Madge and Stan had us ready to go and we jumped to the outskirts of Las Vegas near a huge Las Vegas billboard.

Chapter Three

The cool morning desert air hit my face and I was glad to have the leather jacket on.

Patty had over one shoulder a backpack with three thermoses of hot chocolate, and I had the other backpack on my back with the other three.

Hot chocolate was like an extreme drug to the Silicon Suckers. One single drop of the liquid would send a Sucker into a drug high that seemed to last for a long time.

I had learned a long time ago to never think of going into one of the Silicon Sucker cities without a gift of a thermos of hot chocolate. And since we were going to see the Great One, it made sense to carry even more of the gift.

We had arrived fifteen minutes ahead of our time to meet the Great One, but I had a hunch it would take us that long to get to where he was through the vastness of the underground city. The sun had already lit up the hills and desert with a golden glow and the air still had an early-morning chill to it that promised to be gone very shortly in the summer heat.

"You ready?" I asked.

Patty nodded, but looked very nervous. She had never been inside a Silicon Sucker "sand castle" as they liked to call their huge network of caves and tunnels in the sandstone and rock.

While the hot chocolate was being made, Stan, had briefed Patty on all the rules of the Silicon Sucker city.

We could never touch a wall. We could never sit down unless invited. We had to always treat the Suckers with respect by bowing. We had to give our full and honest name before being allowed to enter. And so on and so on. They were a very rule-bound race.

I had us face directly east, then, to the seemingly open-air twenty paces from the big billboard, I said, "Poker Boy and Front Desk Girl ask for entrance into the great city of the Silicon Suckers."

The entrance of a large tunnel shimmered into existence in front of us. It seemed to go into the side of a hill that just didn't appear to be there. Very weird.

I slipped off my shoes, leaving them on the desert sand. Patty did the same, and we stepped forward into the tunnel that slanted downward gently.

About twenty paces inside we were met by a Silicon Sucker who bowed as we bowed and gave our full names.

"Welcome to our castle once again, Poker Boy," he said. "It is always an honor to have you as a guest."

He turned to Patty. "It is also an honor to have you visit our castle."

"The honor is all mine," Patty said, bowing slightly.

With all the greetings done, the Silicon Sucker turned and indicated we should follow him.

As I had guessed, it seemed to take a long time for us to reach the major cavern and work our way down one wall on sloping ramps. For a person afraid of heights, this path on the face of the wall would be pure hell. It was a long ways down and there were no guardrails and you weren't allowed to touch the wall on the inside.

The cavern seemed to stretch into the distance and the walls were riddled with paths and open tunnels. They seemed to be crawling with Silicon Suckers.

I had never seen so many out and moving at the same time before. I felt like I had been shrunk down and was walking in an anthill.

The floor of the huge cavern had hundreds and hundreds of buildings and I knew from earlier visits that the caverns and tunnels went deep under all the buildings as well.

Seeing so many Silicon Suckers moving at once, I suddenly wondered what all of them ate and how so many could be fed? No doubt I dare not ask such a question.

I glanced at Patty who was following me. She seemed to be doing fine on the wall face, even in the drying air. I could feel the moisture in my lips and skin drying up and the leather jacket I wore didn't feel so comfortable now in the growing heat. But I didn't dare take it off, not only because it would be an insult in the city, but it gave me extra power. And there was no telling what I might need to do in this situation.

The deeper we got into the city, the drier the air got. We could not bring any kind of water with us. Plain drinking water was forbidden in a Silicon Sucker castles.

These places were very, very dangerous to humans. I knew of one superhero who had managed three days in a Silicon Sucker castle negotiating with them on some land swap, but she had barely made it out alive.

We reached the cavern floor and headed toward the huge center building. There was nothing ornate about it and no windows at all. It seemed more like a giant mound of sand. But it was the largest building and it did seem to be in the center of the cavern, which I was sure had some significance.

We were led inside and into a large, domed room with no furniture of any kind. It seemed to be the very center of the large mound of sand that was this building.

The floor was nothing but hard sand, warm under my bare feet, and the walls were brown like everything else in these underground cities. It looked like the special rooms weren't any more decorated than any of the other rooms in this cavern.

The Silicon Sucker who led us into the room indicated we should stand and wait and then he left.

There was only one other door into the room, an archway

on the other side. We both stood, facing that doorway, not talking.

I could feel beads of sweat forming on my face and then drying away almost instantly.

I always got scared inside these cities. After all, Silicon Suckers looked just like every alien I had seen in the movies. That fear was in very deep in all humans, more than likely from centuries around this race.

Honestly, at the moment I was more scared than I had ever been before.

If Laverne had only met the Great One once in thousands of years, why were we standing here?

And how many ways could we make a mistake and never see the light of the desert above again?

Suddenly, in front of us, a Silicon Sucker entered the room completely alone. As with all of them, he wore nothing, but he moved slower than the rest, and as he got closer to us, I could see his bright red eyes. And his face looked longer than the rest. But otherwise, besides the red eyes, I would have never been able to tell the Great One from any other Silicon Sucker.

Patty and I both bowed to him and he returned the bow.

"I thank you for this audience," he said, his voice strong and commanding.

"It is an honor to be asked," I said.

Patty and I both bowed again slightly.

"We have brought gifts, if you would allow us."

He held up his hand for us to not move, and we both stood still.

"I thank you for the gifts," the Great One said, "but I must first talk to you about why I asked you here. My people find themselves in a problem of our own making."

Patty and I carefully said nothing.

"It seems that the gifts you have brought us in the past, and the regular payment for the land we have exchanged, has brought us to a crisis point."

He paused and then looked down as if embarrassed.

I knew he was talking about hot chocolate. Over the last few years I had brought his people six thermoses full. And for a piece of land they were getting ten thermoses every month. I knew that hot chocolate was a very powerful drug to the Silicon Suckers, but I couldn't imagine it becoming a crisis.

Then it hit me. *A powerful drug!*

Could he be mad at me for getting his people hooked on hot chocolate? Had I created a drug problem in his perfectly ordered world? No wonder he wanted to only "talk" with me.

But why had he also asked Patty to come along? Was it because she was special to me and he needed to take something special of mine for what I had done to his people?

I would not allow that.

The Great One looked up at me, the large unblinking red eyes clear.

"Poker Boy," he said, "I do not think you understand the value of your gracious gifts to my people. Your precious gifts give us life and energy. It gives us an excitement that we have not felt in many, many centuries."

I somehow managed to keep my mouth shut and just let him continue. I needed to be ready, if this turned very ugly, to jump Patty and I out of here quickly, or call for Lady Luck to come to our rescue.

The Great One continued.

"Your gifts have allowed me to walk out here without being carried and to stand here as a leader once again."

Now I was staring at him and my eyes suddenly felt like they were as wide as his were.

"Our problem is that our numbers are increasing with the new vitality from your gifts and land payments. And each cycle the payment for the land is not enough to supply my people."

Suddenly the fear I had been feeling turned to barely-controlled panic.

He wasn't mad at me for bringing the gifts of hot chocolate. This was much, much worse.

He needed *more* of it.

Oh, crap. I couldn't just offer it to him as a gift. I would insult him, and more than likely we would die where we stood.

I needed to find a way, and find it quickly, to get the Silicon Suckers more hot chocolate and let the Great One feel as if he was paying a fair price.

I nodded and somehow, keeping my voice from cracking

in the dry air, I said, "A great leader worrying about the well-being of his people. It is an honor to be in your presence."

I took the pack from my shoulder and took out the three thermoses, holding them in my hands and not allowing even the pack to touch the ground.

Beside me, Patty followed my lead and did the same.

"For the honor of meeting with the Great One," I said, "the leader of all Silicon Suckers, we have brought this special gift. I hope it will help while we work out a more lasting solution and a fair and equitable trade."

"I can only thank you for your generosity," he said.

Without any indication of a movement from the Great One, six other Silicon Suckers came out and each took one thermos and carried them away like carrying gold from the room.

After they had left I spoke again.

"May I be so bold as to ask how much of the precious substance is needed to supply the great beings of the race of Silicon Suckers with their needs?"

He stared at me for a moment and I began to wonder if I had gone too far with my question.

Then he said, "We would need four times the amount of your generous gift every moon cycle, plus the payment for the land we are already receiving."

I tried to look serious. Thirty-four thermoses full of hot chocolate. "That is a large amount," I said. "But it is possible. But I must ask for something in return."

"Of course," he said.

I had an idea on what we might trade for, but I had to be very careful in presenting it.

"My people are also in great need in this area for..." I stopped and looked pained. "...I am sorry, I cannot use such language in front of the Great One."

He motioned for me to continue.

"We are in need of plain water. We are a very different people, with different needs. We must have plain water to survive. Is there an area in your lands which is not usable to your people because of too much plain water, that we might trade?"

"Something important to my people in exchange for something important to your people," he said.

I only nodded. Thankfully he saw my purpose and I had not insulted him by asking for what was, in essence, poison to his people.

"Poker Boy, there is a reason my people sing your praises."

"Thank you, Great One," I said.

A map of the area around Las Vegas appeared in the air between us. Some areas were colored in gold for Silicon Sucker lands. Black for human lands. Gray for land that neither party controlled.

I knew the Silicon Suckers protected their own lands fiercely when needed, and no building was allowed within one hundred yards of any border to their property.

Of course, no humans in Las Vegas government knew that. The map had been formed by treaty decades before by the Gods of Land Use and the Silicon Suckers. The Gods in that area made sure nothing was allowed to be built on the Silicon Sucker lands.

The Great One pointed to a small area colored red off to one side of the old Boulder Dam highway. It did not seem to be attached to any other area of Silicon Sucker lands.

"We were forced to abandon a growing castle in this area due to large pools of the evil liquid under the area. I would like five times your most recent gift every moon cycle in trade for the entire area."

He had upped the amount expecting me to bargain. Again, I needed to not insult him by giving in too quickly.

"Forty containers of the precious liquid every moon cycle?" I asked.

He said simply, "Yes."

I pointed at the large area of red off the old highway. "My people will find much of what we need here?"

"You will find much of the poison there," he said.

I didn't want to tell him that the precious liquid he was asking for was based on the poison we called water.

"Twenty-eight additional every moon cycle," I said. "And if we find what we must look for on the land, we will increase the amount to forty total in twelve moon cycles."

He nodded. "Your terms are acceptable."

The red coloring of the land on the map turned to blue and then the map vanished.

"The first payment will be delivered tomorrow morning," I said, "to the area near the entrance to this castle at sunrise, and then at sunrise every moon cycle after."

The Great One bowed and Patty and I bowed also.

"This exchange has given my people a new beginning," he said. "It will allow my people to reproduce and spread and build many large new castles. You will both always be honored guests as long as I rule."

With that he turned and walked away.

For a moment I felt the elation that we had survived the meeting. Then his last words came back strong, like someone was shouting them in my head.

Hot chocolate helped these creatures have baby Silicon Suckers?

Wow, I had not known that. No wonder I had never seen any children. I had never thought of it before.

What had I just done?

Patty and I followed a guide out of the building and back up the wall toward the entrance above. All the paths and tunnels teamed with Silicon Suckers, far, far more than I had ever seen before.

Was all this population growth from just a few thermoses per month of hot chocolate?

Oh, man, what would forty every month do?

What had I done?

Was I setting up a future war between mankind and Silicon Suckers? I sure hoped not.

Outside, after Patty kissed me for a job well done and we put on our shoes in the already hot sun, I told her my worry.

She just laughed in that way she does that makes me relax. It's one of her very special superpowers I'm sure.

Then she said, "I could really use a couple glasses of water and a large breakfast."

"You don't think this is serious, do you?"

"They don't dare expand into our areas and fight with us."

"And why not?" I asked as I jumped us from the hot desert to our favorite booth in the air-conditioning of The Diner. I didn't want to call for Stan and Laverne until I understood what Patty was saying.

"There weren't that many of them moving around last time I was down there," I said as we slid into the booth, the cool vinyl seat feeling wonderful. "That's only after six months of regular hot chocolate use. Imagine after a year?"

Again Patty laughed. "Trust me, they have to treat us well."

"And why?" I asked as Madge headed our way with large glasses of water she must have had ready.

"Because if they don't," Patty said, patting my hand on the table top like I was two years old, "we just cut off their supply of hot chocolate."

"Oh," was all I could think to say.

LIVING TIME

Chapter One

I sat under the gaze of some idiot who had watched too much poker on television as he stared at me like he knew what he was doing. I have no idea what he was looking for, and I had no doubt he didn't know either, but he kept it up, trying to decide if he should toss in his last two hundred bucks and call my bet.

He had on a heavy wool sweater and had taped one side of his glasses with white tape. The longer he stared at me, the more he sweated. He was in the third chair and I was in the sixth. The two men between us had both scooted their chairs back to stay out of the way of the showdown.

Around us the Spirit Winds Casino poker room was doing a good business for ten o'clock on a Thursday night in the middle of January. Five tables were going, including two no-limit tables and from the looks of it there was a waiting list on the board.

The noises from the slots and blackjack tables filtered into the room like a steady background of white noise and two of the televisions in the corners were on, both showing different professional basketball games.

A couple players were sitting at empty tables just watching the games.

I had two more hours before I needed to jump from the Oregon mountains to Las Vegas using my new teleportation power to pick up my girlfriend, Patty Ledgerwood, aka Front Desk Girl, from her job at the MGM Grand Hotel on the Strip. So I was enjoying a friendly game picking up a few hundred here and there along the way.

In two hours it had been a profitable night, a large part because of the guy staring at me. He had started with almost a grand and was down to his last two hundred of the two racks of five-dollar chips he had sat down with.

Outside the Casino the night felt like it would snow at any moment and the wind was biting and cold. In Vegas the temperature would be in the low fifties at midnight when I picked up Patty.

At some point I was going to just move to Vegas, buy or build a place there. But I still liked this casino and the area around it and considered this casino my home casino, even though I didn't spend much times these days in my doublewide trailer a few miles from here.

In fact, I couldn't remember the last night I had slept

there. It hadn't been since Patty and I got more serious and I learned how to teleport. And that had been a good six months.

Down the table the guy just kept watching me, sweating, trying to decide what to do. I had a pair of aces down and there was an ace and two deuces on the board with a king. I doubted he had a pair of deuces in his hand, otherwise he would have called me at once and laughed while flipping his cards over.

More than likely he had the 4th ace and a bad kicker. He might have a king and was wondering if I had an ace. Either way I had him beat and beat badly.

I smiled at him, tipping back my black Fedora-like hat.

"Anything I can tell you?" I asked him, smiling.

The dealer frowned, but said nothing.

The guy just shook his head, checked his cards again, then went back to staring at me.

The more he sweated and stared, the more I stared to sense the guy had a problem larger than this hand. He was playing with money he couldn't afford to lose. I had figured that much out earlier, and now I was about to take his last few hundred. The sweat on his forehead was for a lot more than just a hand and a couple hundred dollars. To this guy, he thought he was betting his entire life.

And at a poker table, that never worked out well. Poker could be a very cruel game, especially when you shouldn't be playing.

He stared and stared, the sweat beading on his forehead

and his eyes slits behind his broken glasses. More than likely he had read some stupid book on poker tells and was trying to watch me for one. So I decided to give him a tell from the first chapter.

I leaned forward, pretending to want to flip my cards over and show him. The book said that if a player acted strong, they had a weak hand. I honestly didn't care if he called me or not. I just wanted the stupid hand over.

He smiled. "You don't have it," he said. "You're bluffing."

He pushed in his last two hundred bucks and then waited for me to flip over my cards. If he had flipped his cards over I might have mucked and just given him the hand and the money, but he didn't.

I flipped over my two aces and his face went pale.

"Might want to read that book again," I said as the dealer shoved the pile of chips my way.

The guy beside the loser on the end of the table just shook his head. "You should know better than to mess with Poker Boy."

I glanced at the guy again, pretending I wasn't upset that he knew my superhero name. But I was.

The dealer glanced at me, then went back to gathering the cards to shuffle.

I didn't like it that someone had used my superhero name here, in my home casino. I didn't like it at all.

I had a read on the guy from his play over the last two hours. Strong player, cautious, no real tells. He was someone to be very careful with. More than likely he was a pro. Of the chips that had come across the table in the last two hours, I had a large number of them and he had the rest.

He wore a tan Izod golf shirt and had put his ski parka on a hook beside the door. He had brown short hair and brown eyes and a slightly hooked nose. He looked to be about thirty, but I could be off in either direction by a decade.

He looked to be about my height at six foot. But he looked stronger, with wider, football-player-like shoulders and neck.

He was nothing exceptional and except for his play, he had stayed under my radar for the two hours he had been at the table. I had just not paid him much attention.

Impressive.

"Have we met?" I asked as I stacked the chips, knowing for a fact that we had never met before. I did not forget a face. I had trouble with names, but never a face. That was part of my superpowers. And as a poker player, I know I would have remembered him from his play.

"Nope," the guy said, smiling. "Stan sent me."

My stomach flipped, but I kept stacking my chips trying to get some sort of read on the situation.

The loser beside him finally decided he was done and shoved his chair back, clearly angry at his loss.

"I hope you two are proud of yourselves," he said looking at me, then at the guy I had been talking to. "I know collusion when I see it."

The guy I had been talking to who claimed Stan had sent him reached over casually and just touched the arm of the guy.

"We're just having a friendly game here," he said. "Nothing out of the ordinary, I can promise you."

The guy sort of stood there for a moment, then shook his head and laughed. "Yeah, I know that. Just sort of mad at my own stupid play."

Wow! The guy had some powers! I was stunned.

"Actually," the guy said to the angry man, "you are pretty damn fine player. You just ran into the best tonight."

The guy nodded. "Thanks, appreciate that." He looked at me, smiled and said, "Nice playing with you."

Then the guy walked off as I stared at the guy who knew my name. I felt I should follow the guy out to see what he planned to do after his loss, but at that moment I was more concerned with the guy across from me who knew my name.

"You said Stan sent you?" I asked. "Which Stan?"

"Your boss of course," the guy said, smiling.

CHAPTER TWO

I instantly took the two of us out of time, freezing everyone else in the room. All the sounds of the casino vanished and everyone stayed in place, stuck between two moments in time.

Except the two of us.

"Wow, nifty trick," the guy said, his eyes large as he looked around. "I hope I can learn how to do that someday."

"Stan!" I shouted at the ceiling as I stood and moved a few steps away from the poker table.

A moment later Stan, the God of Poker, appeared in front of me. He was wearing his normal tan slacks, tan shirt and sweater and he was smiling.

"Good," he said to me. "I see you've met The Kid. How'd he do?"

"What do you mean by that?"

Stan smiled and looked at the chips in front of both of our chairs. "Doesn't look like he got much of your money."

"He's a fine player," I said. "I just want to know how he knows me and you?"

"I'm right here, guys," The Kid said, waving his hand.

Stan laughed. "He's the new recruit. So how did he do?"

"Besides blurting out my name in front of an entire table, and mentioning your name, and being way too old to be called kid, he played decent poker."

Stan looked at The Kid and shook his head. "You never say another superhero's name out loud in front of regular people."

"Sorry," The Kid said, actually looking worried and sheepish. "I didn't know."

Stan laughed and waved it off. "You'll learn."

I couldn't begin to count the times Stan had used those same words with me in my first few years as a superhero. And now that I was actually looking at The Kid, he did look a lot younger than my first take on his age. At most he was twenty-five. It was a nifty trick being able to shift his age appearance like that. I would have to learn it.

"New recruit?" I asked Stan. "Working for you?"

"Yup," Stan said, smiling. "Laverne approved it and everything. She said you and your team are doing more work for all of the Gods and I needed the help with just poker."

"I told you that last week," I said, smiling at him.

I walked over to The Kid and stuck out my hand as he stood from the table. "Nice meeting you, Kid."

"The honor is all mine, Poker Boy," The Kid said, smiling and shaking my hand like I was a rock star. "You are the smoothest player I have ever had the honor to sit with."

"You ain't half bad yourself," I said. "And nice job staying hidden as long as you did."

"Thanks," he said, beaming.

I remembered in my early years how important it was to have someone tell me I did something right. Hell, after ten years now, it was still important. I doubt it would ever get old.

Then I got serious as I turned back to Stan. "I can handle it from here," I said. "We have some work to do."

"Give him time," Stan said to me. "Don't push too hard."

"I promise," I said.

Stan vanished and I turned back to The Kid. "Come with me. We have a problem to clean up."

The kid looked puzzled, but followed me through the frozen people and the silence of the casino.

"This is just creepy," he said, staring at a woman chewing on a large hotdog, her mouth open and full of half-eaten bun.

About halfway across the casino I found who I was looking for. The guy who had been at the table on that last hand. I had taken the last of his money.

"Did you sense any problem with this guy?" I asked The Kid.

"He was desperate, playing with important money. That's why I tried to calm him some."

"And you did fine with that, but my sense is that what you did won't be enough. I may be wrong, but if I'm not, I want to make sure nothing goes too wrong."

The Kid looked puzzled, but only nodded.

"Now, let's get back to the table so I can put us in real time again. Follow my lead."

CHAPTER THREE

When we were both seated, I put us back into the nature flow of time. The sounds of the casino smashed into us.

"Let's go talk," I said to The Kid and pushed my chair back.

"Glad to," he said. Then to the dealer he said, "We'll be right back."

The dealer nodded and began dealing to the other six at the table.

The Kid stayed with me as we left the poker room.

"Dead camera area here," I said and jumped us to a dead camera area in the parking lot.

The Kid looked stunned. "Wow, do I have a lot to learn."

"Give it time," I said, heading toward the front door of the casino.

A moment later the guy who had tried to get a read on me came out of the front door and turned to the left toward one of the parking lots. When he got there, he climbed into an old Ford that looked like it had seen its better days.

Then he just sat behind the wheel as if he had no place to go.

More than likely, if my sense of him was right, he didn't.

The Kid and I stood off to one side near a truck so we could watch him and not be seen. I had on my black leather coat and hat that was my superhero uniform, but I could still feel the cold wind. The Kid was in a short-sleeved golf shirt and he was shaking already.

"You might want to learn to always wear a jacket of some sort in a poker room," I said. "Both for sitting under air-conditioning and for this job."

"I'll remember that," he said, his teeth almost chattering.

"Where you from?" I asked.

"Southern California," he said.

"You want to go back in for your coat?"

He shook his head. "I'll make it."

At that moment the guy in the car moved. But he didn't go to turn on his car. Instead, he reached over to his glove box and opened it and pulled out what looked to be a pistol of some type.

"Shit, he's going to off himself," The Kid said, starting to run at the car.

I jumped us out of time again, then called for The Kid to hold on. He stopped and waited for me.

"I really need to learn how to do that," he said.

Then he followed me over to the car as I opened the car door, took the gun from the guy's hand, unloaded the clip, made sure there was no round anywhere in the gun, then put the gun back in the guy's hand, closed the door and indicated that The Kid should follow me away from the car.

"You were sure right about the guy," he said. "How did you know?"

"Just reading people," I said.

We got back to where we had been and I let us go back into the flow of time. The wind again hit us hard and The Kid shivered.

"Follow my lead completely," I said and he nodded as we started back toward the guy's car.

He didn't see us coming. He just kept staring at the gun in his hands until I knocked on the window and startled him.

He tried to hide the gun by dropping it on the floor before he opened the car door and stepped out into the cold.

"Yeah," he said. "So you two really are together."

"Not really," I said. "In fact, we just met tonight at the table, but we were both worried about you."

"You are the only people on the planet who are," he said, the sarcasm clear in his voice. "Thanks."

He was in even worse shape than I thought.

I turned on what I call my "empathy-power" and directed it at the guy. And also the power I call "tell-me-the-truth." With both of those powers directed at the poor guy, he had no choice but tell me what was going on like I was a trusted counselor he had poured his heart out to for years.

"So how bad is it?" I asked. "What's happening?"

"No job, my wife left me six months ago, I'm homeless, and you took the last of my money. I don't even have gas money to get off this stupid mountain and back to Portland. That's how bad."

"That's bad," I said, nodding.

Beside me The Kid nodded, but said nothing.

"So what did you do for a living?" I asked.

He laughed. "What every other unemployed person around this area did. I worked construction. Actually, I had my own construction business, had a dozen guys working for me, building some of the best custom homes in Oregon. Bobby C. Davis Construction."

He said the name of his business with pride and I suddenly had a great idea to help this guy not put the barrel of that gun in his mouth.

I laughed. "Great meeting you," I said and extended my hand. "I'm Gary Barnes."

Gary Barnes was one of my fake names I used in the real world when I had to. Actually, everyone around this casino called me Gary and my doublewide trailer a couple miles away was under that name as well.

The kid stepped forward to shake the guy's hand. "I'm Roger Stevens," he said.

I had a hunch that was a made-up name by The Kid as well.

"Bob Davis," the guy said, now even more puzzled.

I kept the empathy power turned on high and focused at him and then also turned on my "trust-me" power. This poor guy was putty in my hands, especially in his depressed condition. Luckily, I only used my powers for good.

"I actually looked for your business a few months back," I said, lying through my teeth. I was a poker player. Lying was part of our job description. "I've been wanting to build a custom home on some property I have near here, a big, beautiful custom home, and your firm was recommended to me a number of times."

"Really?" he asked, smiling. Then his mood turned again. "See how quality work turns out?" He pointed at the old car he was driving. "I sold my rig and most of my tools to get living money and money to pay my child support. I hoped to win enough tonight to make next month's payment and get a little apartment. That went well as you know."

"How old are your children?" The Kid asked, expertly moving the subject from the guy's loss to something better.

The guy seemed to melt at the mention of them. "Six and eight," he said.

"I think they would rather have their father than money," I said.

He shrugged, but I could tell he wasn't so sure.

CHAPTER FOUR

"Tell you what, Bob," I said. "How about you go to work for me and my girlfriend and build us the house of our dreams?" I sure hoped Patty had some idea of what would make a good custom home. I didn't.

He looked at me and then smiled, but shook his head. "I don't have the tools or even a truck or a place to stay."

"None of that's a problem," I said, laughing. "I need someone with your skill. I've got a doublewide close to here that I'm not using that you can live in for free, and I'll fund you for a new truck and tools. Besides that, I'll put you on a regular salary for as long as it takes to build the house. And from what Patty and I want, that might take some time. All custom."

We all three stood there in the cold wind as he again stared at me, again trying to get a read on me.

Luckily, this time it didn't take as long as at the poker table.

"Are you for real?" he asked. "You can't really be scamming me. I've got nothing more anyone could take."

"I'm not kidding," I said. "I was hoping to hire someone with your skill to build me a house here and from the looks of your situation, I can get you cheaper than you used to charge. A good deal for me."

With that he laughed. "Yeah, a bunch cheaper, to be honest."

"Do we have a deal?" I asked, extending my hand. "You come to work for me and build me the best damn place you can. And maybe by the time you're done, the economy will have turned a little and you can ramp your business back up. Or come down to Vegas and help me build a house there after you're are done here."

He hesitated for only a moment, looking me right in the eyes, and then he nodded and shook my hand, smiling. "We have a deal. Thanks. You need to know you just saved my life."

"Actually," I said, waving off his thank you. "You just saved me from moving away from a place I love. But we have to make one more agreement."

"What's that?" he asked, looking suddenly worried.

"You won't come in here while you work for me to do anything but have dinner. You're a fine poker player, but you need to play for the right reasons."

"Deal," he said, smiling. "And after we get the house done, maybe you can give me some lessons."

"That I can do," I said, smiling.

I handed him a few hundred dollars and pointed at the gas station and grocery across the highway. "This is an advance. I'm going to go cash out my chips. You need to get some gas and some food to stock a fridge for later and breakfast. There's not a damn thing in that doublewide. Meet me back here in twenty minutes."

"Got it, boss," he said, smiling, the look of desperation now completely gone from his eyes, replaced with a glimmer of hope.

Halfway back across the cold parking lot, The Kid finally broke his silence. "That felt great helping him like that. Is that what it's like being a superhero?"

"Sometimes, yeah, it is. On the good nights."

We walked a little ways in silence again before he asked the next question.

"You really wanted to build a house up here?"

I laughed. "I hadn't actually thought of it until tonight. But I own some nice land on hills around here as well as my doublewide. And Patty, my girlfriend, won't stay up here with me because my place is so shabby. So I might as well build a house with her help so she'll come up here at times."

"You like it here that much?" The Kid asked as we got close to the front doors.

"I do," I said.

"So you saved a man's life and helped yourself at the same time. You are good. Both at poker and at life."

"Is there much difference?" I asked, repeating a phrase that Stan once said to me when I was starting out.

"Not when you play them both the way you do," The Kid said, holding the front door of the Casino open for me.

And that was one of the nicest things anyone had said to me in a long time. I was going to like this kid.

DEAD EVEN

DEAD EVEN

Bob showed up in the poker room at Spirit Winds Casino on Christmas Eve. Bob, like his name, was a very short man. I guessed he came up to my shoulder at best, even with heels on his boots. It's always interesting to me how names fit people. Bob fit Bob perfectly.

His black hair was short, the nails on his fingers were trimmed short, and even his nose was short. He wore a golf shirt that seemed a size too small, and brown slacks that covered brown dress shoes. He did not have the appearance of having money, but over the years I have come to not trust appearances very much, since I look like a slob most of the time, yet I have money and am a super hero.

In looks, I am, for lack of a better way of putting it, the cliché white male. I'm six feet tall, have brown hair that's graying slightly at the temples, and green eyes. Bob was the cliché short man who walked quick, talked quick, and had a flaring temper that might go off with just a wrong remark, or more likely, a bad beat at the table.

Cliché meet cliché.

Bob took every turn of the cards as if it was more than just a bad beat. He seemed to take it as an affront to his height. A ten would hit the table to give someone else a pair of tens to beat his pocket nines, and he acted if someone had just called him a runt.

It was a guaranteed way to lose money at a poker table.

Bad beats at poker tables are when a person thinks they should win, but the cards at the end of the hand say otherwise. Every poker player I know tells bad beat stories about how his pocket aces were beaten by jack/ten suited. Bad beats are the nature of poker, and I put them on people as often as people put them on me, so I pay no attention. Someone starts into a bad beat story and I just nod and think about what I'm planning on having for dinner.

All night long Bob kept complaining, and then continuing to play. He wasn't a bad player, but he wasn't a good one either. He knew just enough to think he was the best, and just enough to think he knew what he was doing, and just enough to think he could beat me and the rest of the group at the table. Of course he was wrong on all three counts. And he complained about it bitterly.

Clearly short Bob was not a happy man, either in poker or in life.

The turning point of the evening came when Bob had

aces beat twenty minutes before midnight on Christmas Eve. He stared at the aces, then at the winning flush a guy named Carl had drawn into, then at the dealer, and for a moment I thought he was going to punch the dealer.

Now understand, during the evening so far, he had lost upwards of a three grand in just under five hours, with about half of it sitting safely in the stack of chips in front of me. However, it was not my flush that had just put the bad beat on his aces.

I'm Poker Boy, and Christmas Eve or not, I played fair, and if someone wanted to give me their money across a poker table, I took it. There is no Santa in a poker game, but good old short Bob sure wanted to give me his money, so I was thinking kindly of him at that moment, even with him yelling at the dealer and complaining all the time.

I'm not sure yelling describes what Bob was actually doing. He was ranting, screaming, shouting, and even foaming at the mouth a little. He had stood up and was even leaning over the table. For a tall man, this might have been threatening. For Bob, it made no difference.

The rake, a guy named Henry, watches over the dealers in a poker room. Henry came over and asked Bob to calm down. All the while the dealer named Scooter just sat there, staring ahead, ignoring Bob's ranting and shouting and carrying on.

"I'm not going to calm down!" Bob shouted.

At this point, Krissy, the room manager on duty showed up at the table. She was about Bob's height, with long blonde hair and a smile that could fill a room.

Scooter kept ignoring Bob, shuffled up, and got ready to deal the next hand.

"What's the problem?" Krissy asked Bob, as if she didn't know exactly what the problem was.

"Your dealer's cheatin' me!" Bob turned and shouted right into her face. Then he stepped toward her.

I just sat there watching. These situations were not the things that Poker Boy got involved with. My job was to save helpless people and dogs, not stop idiots from making fools of themselves.

Besides, Krissy was one tough broad who had many different colored belts from different martial arts disciplines. If Bob was stupid enough to take a swing at Krissy, he would be lucky to see it turn Christmas day.

"Our dealers do not cheat, sir," Krissy said, her voice low and level as she spoke right into Bob's face. "And we have cameras to make sure they don't."

"I don't care about no damned cameras!" Bob shouted. "For all I know, the dealer and the camera man are in this together."

I glanced around at the other seven players on the table. All of us had some of this idiot's money. Did he think we were all in on his great conspiracy as well? Of course, I didn't say that. Instead the rest of us just sat there as if nothing was happening, staring at either our hands, the felt tabletop, or the wall beyond the table. The number one rule when there's a problem at a poker table was to stay out of it.

"I think maybe a little walk might calm you down," Krissy

said, moving to take Bob's elbow and turn him from the table.

"I don't need a walk!" Bob shouted, his face really red.

The next chain of events happened quickly.

Bob went to shove Krissy aside.

Krissy grabbed Bob's arm.

Bob tried to push Krissy.

Krissy moved a step out of the way, grabbing Bob in such a way that the man sort of lifted off the ground using his own forward motion, flew through the air with Krissy still holding on, and then came down flat, face first, on the empty table beside the one we were playing on.

Krissy now held Bob's arm behind his back with one hand and the back of his neck with the other, acting as if she had to do this every day.

Bob kicked for a moment trying to break free, but it looked like with each kick, he hurt himself, so he stopped.

Man, I was going to have to get to know Krissy better. She might come in handy as a sidekick on some of my adventures. Sure, I had super powers and all that, but sometimes a good hand-to-hand fighting master could beat a super power in the clinch.

"Deal this man out," Krissy said. She didn't seem excited or even winded. "And cash in his chips and give him his money."

Henry, the rake, moved to take what was left of Bob's chips. More than likely his anger had just saved him the last of his money.

A moment later, two large security men came in the poker room door, handcuffed Bob, and started to lead him away, with Henry carrying Bob's money right behind.

"Wait!" Bob shouted. "I have to stay. I have to win enough!"

Suddenly my Poker Boy alarm went off. I sometimes call this alarm my Ultra-Intuition Power. And right now that power was telling me in no uncertain terms that Bob needed my help, and not to escape the security guards.

I got up, leaving my chips on the table, and followed Bob, the guards, and Henry the rake. It felt as if we were having a little parade as the crowds parted to let us through.

The two large security men, with Bob walking between them like a small child being escorted to the principal's office, headed for the front door of the casino. When they had him safely out on the sidewalk and the handcuffs off, Henry gave Bob the remaining money and went back inside.

"Please don't return to this casino, sir," one big guard said.

"You're lucky Krissy's not going to press charges against you," the other said.

Bob just nodded, standing there in the cold evening air, the last of his money in his hand. He looked to be completely in shock and beaten, as if his world had just ended. Clearly he must have been playing poker with scared money, and the worst way to ever play poker is with scared money.

Scared money means the money you are using is not money you can afford to lose. You never gamble with rent or food or car payment money. Never. Ever. Only gamblers with problems do that.

"Where's your car, Bob?" I asked, stepping up between him and the guards and taking his arm. I turned him gently toward the closest parking lot.

"Around on the other side of the building," Bob said.

"I'll walk you," I said, glad I always wore my black leather coat and Fedora-like hat when playing, since we were going to have to go around the building and it was a cold Christmas Eve. It wasn't snowing or anything, but it felt cold enough to.

We walked in silence for a hundred yards or so, then finally Bob said softly, "I knew better."

"I know you did," I said. "How much did you need to win?"

"Six over the top of the four I had," he said, without looking at me.

We kept walking in silence, our breathing making frost waves ahead of us in the parking lot lights.

Now a couple times a year I have nights in live games where I win far over six thousand. And I've won numbers of tournaments with payouts a great distance over six thousand. But I doubted Bob had ever won that much in a casino, so whatever had made him try this stupidity on Christmas Eve had to be very important to him.

I clicked on my special Empathy Power.

To be honest, I just don't know what else to call the power. It makes people believe they can tell me anything, trust me with their very lives. And sometimes they do. But

Empathy is the wrong name for it, but Trust Me Power just doesn't sound right. And neither does Make Them Talk Power. I'd figure it out some day.

With my Empathy Super Power on, I asked the next question. "Bob, what did you need the money for?"

Bob glanced at me. "What do you care?"

I notched up my Empathy Power. Little Bob needed a big dose. "Trust me, I care," I said, staring right at him to focus the strength.

He shrugged. "You wouldn't believe me if I told you."

I turned up the Empathy Power to the top of my capabilities and focused it at him like I was staring at a fly. Bob stood no chance. He was going to tell me.

"You would be surprised what I would *believe*," I said.

He shrugged. "I wanted to die even."

Now, of all the reasons he could have told me he wanted ten thousand dollars, that was not one I expected. I wouldn't have been surprised at his daughter needing an operation, or his needing to replace money he took from his wife to bet on the horses, or maybe even he needed to buy a girlfriend a new sports car.

"You're going to have to explain that one," I said, keeping my Empathy Power cranked up.

"Christmas morning at six-ten," Bob said, his voice level and matter-of-fact. "Not long from now, actually, I'm going to die."

"And how do you know that?" I asked, even more stunned.

"I told you that you wouldn't believe me."

"Oh, I believe you," I said. "I'm just wondering how you know, or are you planning this exit from the here-and-now."

I really didn't want to spend Christmas Eve babysitting a short guy who wanted to kill himself because his life sucked and he was a bad poker player. I would do it to save his life, but I didn't want to.

He laughed, the sound echoing over the frost-covered cars as we headed down a row, clearly getting closer to his car.

"Not planning a thing," he said. "In fact, I wish I could stay around long enough to learn how to play poker like you do."

"But, you're not?" I said, ignoring his complement.

"Nope." He glanced at his watch. "About six hours from now I'll be as dead as they come. I just know it, like I know the sun is going to come up tomorrow, and the tide is going to change. Call it a special power of mine. Most people never understand that I get these feelings about things, so a long time ago I quit telling people."

I knew that feeling. I dropped my Empathy Power and focused another of my super powers on him to see if he was telling me the truth.

After a moment I realized he seemed to be.

"All right," I said, "I buy that you think you're going to die in about six hours. And you need the ten grand to pay off one last debt?"

"Naw," he said. "Actually I got a bunch of money in stocks, good equity in my house, and both cars paid off. But when I add up the worth of everything, now that the market is down, the balance owed on my house is ten thousand over what I got in assets. I wanted to leave this life even, just like I came in. It seems that's too much to ask, isn't it?"

Again he laughed and stopped beside a late model SUV. For such a little guy, he sure drove a big, expensive car.

"You got a wife and kids?" I asked, still not completely clear on why this guy wanted ten thousand.

"Sure do," Bob said, smiling. "She's back in Minnesota visiting family, and both my kids are grown and married. They are both with their spouse's families this year."

"They left you alone?"

"I wanted them to," he said. "I sort of set it up, and let me tell you, it took some convincing. But I figured why have them hanging around when this heart of mine lets go? It's going to be hard enough on them as it is."

I nodded, not knowing exactly what to say. Either they watched him die, or they got a phone call saying that he was dead. I honestly didn't know which was worse either. But Bob clearly knew for him and his family, and I gave him that.

"Well, it was good playing cards with you," Bob said. "A real pleasure to get beaten by one of the best."

He beeped his SUV unlocked and opened the big door, getting ready to climb inside. I couldn't just let him go off like this, especially since I knew he was telling the truth.

"Bob, wait," I said. "I'm a gambling man, I'll make you a wager. How much do you have left?"

He reached into his pocket and pulled out the bills Henry had given him, made a quick count. "About a grand."

"All right, I'll give you ten to one odds you don't die this morning. If you do, you have ten thousand from me and go out even, if you don't, I get your thousand."

He stared at me for the longest time. Then he asked, "Why would you do that?"

I shrugged. "I'm a gambler. It sounds like a safe way to get that last thousand of yours, since you won't give it to me at the table."

An aside. Actually, I'm not a gambler. In fact, I never play if I don't have what's called "the-best-of-it." I never bet slots, or any other house game where the odds are in favor of the house. I am a poker player, and in poker, skill is everything. And since I'm one of the best in the country, I usually get the best of other people.

But tonight, I placed a bet to help someone.

Again he sort of stared at me for a moment. Then he said, "You're not kidding, are you?"

"Nope," I said. I dug into my pocket and brought out a roll of bills and counted off ten big ones.

I usually carry about twenty thousand in cash on me when I'm headed into a poker room. Then, no matter the size of the game I find, I can handle the buy-in. It never occurs to me that most people would be scared to death walking around with that much cash. I'm a super hero, so I don't have a lot of worries about getting mugged.

"Give me your card," I said.

I figured him for a businessman, and every businessman I knew had a card, and he was no exception.

He dug it out of his wallet and handed it to me.

"Robert Day," I said. "Portland, Oregon. That's you and a current phone number?"

"It is," he said, nodding.

"And this is your car?" I asked.

"It is," he said.

I went around back and recorded the licensee plate number of the big SUV, then moved back to where he stood.

"Here's the deal," I said, talking quick so he didn't have a chance to say anything. "I give you the ten thousand right now. You go home, do what you had planned on doing tonight, and if you're dead in the morning, the money is yours. If your fear is wrong, and you live through the morning, you come back here tomorrow night at eight and give me my ten grand back, plus one thousand of your own money."

He sort of stood there, his mouth open.

I knew I was just giving him the money. This was the biggest sham bet ever come up with, and I was doing my best to sell it to him. But I knew I had lost the ten big ones if he took this, and I didn't care.

An aside. Bob was a real jerk, of that I had no doubt, but he was a jerk who needed my help, and just because someone was a jerk, that didn't mean I shouldn't help that jerk.

I held up the card and smiled. "I know where you live. And I figure I can trust you. Just don't go offing yourself to win this."

At that he laughed. "Are you kidding? I'd love to come back here tomorrow, give you your money and a thousand, and buy you a drink. If they let me back in the casino, that is."

"I'll set it up so they will," I said. "But I doubt they're going to let you play poker for a while."

"Not a problem there," he said, laughing. "I needed my head examined to go up against the likes of you and the others at that table."

"So do we have a bet?" I asked, still shoving my sham bet, which was the only way I knew how to help him.

He again looked at me for the longest time. I had long ago turned off my Empathy Power, and I can't read minds, so I had no idea why he just sort of stared at me.

Then he stuck out his hand. "We have a bet."

His handshake was firm and quick, as you would expect from someone who moved and acted like Bob.

I handed him the ten thousand.

He handed me back one thousand of it. "Nine-to-one odds," he said. "I only need ten thousand total to be even in life, and I have one thousand already."

"Even better," I said.

Did I mention I wasn't a gambler? I could figure the math of a poker hand to exact figures, but a sham bet like this one, I had no clue.

"Thanks," he said, staring at the money. "I don't know why this is so important to me. Seems silly, actually, now that I think about it. No one's going to care that I went out even except me, and I'll be dead."

"Just make sure you're back here tomorrow night with my money. My nine and your grand. I'm going to collect on that drink as well."

"If I'm alive, I'll be here," he said. "Thank you."

With that he got into his big SUV and started it up. He backed out, and with a blink of his lights, drove off.

I went back inside, got myself a large mug of hot chocolate to cut the chill, and went back to the table. I had just given a guy nine thousand dollars to make him feel better during the last few hours of his life. I had no doubt he was going to die, just as he said he would. I had the same power he had, only I called my power Precog-Power.

He was going to die at the exact moment he told me he was, from a massive heart attack. Not even being in a hospital would change the result, that much I was sure of. Otherwise I would have been working to get him to one.

No, the only thing I could do for him was help him make his goal of going out the same way he came into the world: Dead even.

It cost me nine thousand, but what the hell, it was Christmas.

I waited around the next night at eight, just in case we were both wrong. He didn't show, and by midnight, in a very good game, I had won most of my money back.

His death was reported in the paper the next day, exactly as we had both known it would be.

Two weeks later, a very short man came into the casino poker room asking for me. He looked like a younger and shorter version of Bob. He handed me an envelope with nine thousand in it.

The guy looked puzzled, then said simply, "My father willed this to you. Said it had to be cash and left instructions that I was to buy you a drink after I gave it to you. And never play poker with you."

I laughed and steered Bob Junior out of the poker room and toward the bar. On the way he asked, "How well did you know my father?"

"Not that well," I said. "Played some cards with him is all, but I liked him. An honest man."

"That he was," his son said, smiling. "That he was."

LUCK BE A LADY

CHAPTER ONE

One night, while playing in a great, no-limit game, I was asked if I believed in luck. I said, "Sure, I've met her." That got a laugh and the subject changed.

Now understand that professional poker players like me tend to really downplay the factor of luck in our sport, using the great old saying, "It will all even out."

I have to admit that I agree with that, even though I sometimes wonder why luck exists at all when a bad player hits a two-outer to beat me out of few hundred bucks. Particularly when I know I had the best hand going to the last card, and ninety-four-point-four percent of the time I will win that same hand. Correct as far as the math goes, but not very comforting as I watch the idiot player pull my money toward him.

Most people would say in those circumstances that I was unlucky and the idiot was lucky. I never looked at it that way. I just repeated, "It will all even out," as if I didn't really believe in luck.

I have to admit, I've hit my share of two-outers over the years against other players, but as Poker Boy, one of the only superheroes in the Poker World, I try not to get into hands where the only way I can win is hit one of two cards left in the deck that could win the hand for me. It is just too embarrassing.

So, do I actually believe in luck? Like I said, sure. I've met her. And I'm not kidding. And she scared hell out of me.

Her name is Laverne, and she runs everything. She's the top Gambling God, the CEO of all gambling of all types, including risks in business, health, sports, and life in general. She's the one woman in the world you would not want mad at you.

I met her right after the big problems with the Ghost Slot machines. She is what you would imagine Lady Luck to be: short, but powerful, brown hair pulled back, with brown eyes that see through everything. She is completely in control of all the Gods of Gambling. She flat scared me speechless when she thanked Front Desk Girl, my sidekick, and me. She said we did a "damn fine" job in rescuing the gambling industry. Then she smiled.

Those who wish "Lady Luck to smile on them" have never actually had it happen. I was trembling so hard that all I could do was nod and just try to stammer out a "Thanks."

Stan, the God of Poker and my boss, later told me I did just fine. He told me he gets scared every time he has to meet Laverne as well. Usually he just reports to Burt, the God of Casino Operations, who is his boss and second in command of all Gambling Gods under Laverne.

I had hoped to never have a reason to meet Laverne again. I had no idea how long superheroes in the gambling industry lived, but no matter how long it was going to be for me, I did not want to end up in that office of hers again. However, like any poker player, I kept hoping she would "smile" on me every so often from a distance, especially when I stumbled into one of those two-outer situations on the wrong side.

But distance from Lady Luck wasn't to be an option for me.

It was a calm Christmas Eve.

Christmas Eve always tends to bring me strange problems to solve, weird people to rescue, and once even an old girl-friend with new boobs that she thought aliens wanted. So, wouldn't you just know that it would be on Christmas Eve that the biggest problem of my short 42 years would come calling.

It was around six-thirty, and I had just finished some darned fine turkey with dressing and gravy in the casino buffet, after which I sat down in a really nice three/five no limit cash game. I lived in a manufactured home about a half-mile from the Native American casino I liked to call my "home casino." and when home I always ate at the casino, usually in the buffet. For some reason, the cooks there were just better than even my ability to microwave a Hungry Man dinner.

On Christmas Eve in a casino, it is usually only the hard-core players, and this Christmas was no exception. About fourteen guys and two women crowded around two of the eleven poker tables. I would have bet that not a one of us had much family, and clearly none of us had anything better to do on a very cold and damp Tuesday night in December in Oregon.

I had just picked up a pair of nines in late position behind three players who had already limped in. There was just not much for me to do with those cards in that position except call and hope to hit a set. If I tried raising with the nines, anyone who would call me would surely have me beat. But if I got in cheap and hit a third nine on the flop, I could make a bunch of money. So, as I tossed a five dollar chip out in front of me, I felt a hand on my shoulder and glanced up.

It was Stan, the God of Poker.

Now, the last thing you need on a calm Christmas Eve after a good turkey dinner is the God of Poker standing behind you not looking happy. All I could think about was that I had somehow screwed up rescuing that woman with big hair and an even bigger dog a few days before. I had managed to get her professional help right before she started stealing funds from the school where she was the bookkeeper to pay for her poker debt. She was, without a doubt, the worst poker player I had ever met. Everything she knew about the game she had learned by watching late night poker on television. To her, a seven-deuce off-suit was as powerful as a pair of kings, and she always got angry when she lost with that combination, which was most every time she played.

I just hoped she wasn't back in a poker room again.

"After the hand," Stan said, "a word."

Everyone at the table glanced up at Stan, then just looked away. They had no idea who they were looking at, and that he was the guy they were always asking for help or being angry at. More than likely Stan had some sort of "don't pay attention to me" shield up.

I nodded, glanced back at the flop to see that no nine had hit the table, then stood, leaving my cards face down in front of my spot with a nod at the dealer to fold them out when it came around to my turn. I quickly grabbed my chips and stuffed them in my pocket. If Stan had come to get me, chances are it was going to be a little while before I returned to the game.

I zipped up my superhero uniform as I followed Stan toward the poker room front door. My uniform is a short, black leather jacket and a fedora-like golf hat. Both allow me to take my superhero energy from any casino I am in or near. I had a hunch that Stan coming to get me meant I was going to need just about all my powers. In all the years I had worked for him, he had never done this.

Ever.

Normally I just stumbled into the people who needed my help. And if I needed to talk to Stan, I went to find him.

Something was really wrong.

As we stepped out of the poker room and into the larger casino area, my hometown casino just faded away and I suddenly found myself in Stan's office. Out his big picture window, the lights of Vegas lit up the Christmas Eve sky. I loved Vegas. I just hadn't expected to be here at the moment.

And I didn't expect Patty Ledgerwood, a.k.a. Front Desk Girl, to stand and greet me as well. She looked like she had just come from a corporate business meeting, with a fashionable brown suit and slacks over a white blouse. Simple pearls were all that she wore for jewelry, and she had her long brown hair down and combed perfectly. Stunning was the only way to describe her, and my breath just caught in my throat like I had caught a pair of aces playing head's up late in a tournament.

She gave me a huge and long hug, and I have to admit, I returned the hug, getting lost in her long brown hair and her wonderful smell of apricots. Since the big affair with the Ghost Slots, Patty and I had been an item, a couple, good friends, and great partners in a number of other adventures. Clearly Stan figured whatever was wrong was going to need us both again.

"Merry Christmas," she said, giving me that beaming smile that made my knees weak as she pushed me out to arm's length. For a moment I got lost in her big brown eyes, then she kissed me.

Right there in front of the God of Poker.

I didn't care. I kissed her back. Christmas Eve was looking up, that was for sure.

Suddenly I wished I hadn't zipped up my leather jacket. Warm wasn't half of what I was feeling right at that moment.

"Excuse me," Stan said, dropping into his chair with a look of amusement on his face as we pulled apart, "but we have a problem that could use you two."

He pointed to the chairs in front of his desk and we sat. But I didn't let go of her hand. Patty and I had a real connection, even so much that at we could stop time around us, using parts of both of our powers to do it. Besides, I just liked the feel of her skin against mine and couldn't believe a woman as good-looking as she was would even be interested in a poker player like me.

"Okay, right to the point," Stan said, suddenly very serious. "Laverne is missing."

That was such a stupid statement, I just snorted, not a very appealing sound, but one that suited such an absurd statement.

"Now, seriously," Patty said, letting go of my hand and leaning in toward Stan. "What exactly is going on?"

Stan didn't blink, and I couldn't get a read on him in any way. He was the God of Poker after all, and had the best poker face that ever existed.

"Not kidding, I'm afraid," he said. "Laverne has gone missing. As of two hours and six minutes ago real time, there has been no such thing as luck, either good or bad, in the world."

Patty opened her pretty mouth, then closed it without saying a word. I just sat back and stared at Stan. There was no reason at all he would play some sort of prank on us on Christmas Eve, let alone suggest such a thing as Lady Luck herself being missing. Such a thing could get even the God of Poker fired.

But to be honest, in my lowly position as a superhero in the gambling world, I had no idea who might be more powerful than Laverne. I had heard about Karen, Stew, and Mickey, the Gods of Death, Dying, and Spirits; but unless Laverne's time had come to leave this planet, I couldn't imagine those three being involved.

And way back in time there used to be a guy called Zeus who had other names down through time, but he was officially retired and out of the game.

Hell, Laverne had been around since the time of the Greeks and way before.Over the centuries she had taken over all of gambling. From what I had heard, she had gained power over the last few centuries until she was now one of the most powerful of them all. Even all the sports gods, financial gods, and health gods now reported to her.

About the only gods who outranked her now were The Powers That Be and the Fates. I had no doubt that someone far above me would be contacting them pretty soon, if this didn't get cleared up.

"Why do you say missing?" Patty asked. "Did she maybe just go on vacation?"

"My bosses are calling it a kidnapping," Stan said. "But I'm not so sure about that. She is missing and they are panicked, to be honest with you. Even the Fates are stumped.

And since you two did such a good job on the Ghost Slot problem, Burt wants you both in on this as well, even though every God above you is also working on this."

"You don't expect much out of us, I hope," I said.

He shrugged but didn't disagree. Always better to keep a boss's expectations low; then when something works out, you look even better.

I wanted to ask him what he thought a couple of lowly superheroes could do to find Lady Luck herself. Stan knew the odds, and without luck playing a part in anything at the moment, it was only odds that ruled the world. Simple odds. And the odds in this case were not with Patty and me.

Suddenly it dawned on me what I had thought.

Odds.

I needed someone to compute straight computer odds on exactly where Laverne might be, and I knew exactly who could do it.

I sat back, thinking, as Patty asked Stan another question.

"What's going to happen to the world without luck?" Patty asked.

"No one really knows," Stan said. "It's been a part of human nature since the beginning of time."

"I'm betting it's going to get real boring," I said.

Patty and Stan both nodded to that.

CHAPTER TWO

One hour later, Patty and I sat in a small diner just down the street from Binion's Hotel and Casino in downtown Las Vegas. One street over, the light show along Freemont was going full force for those out on Christmas Eve, but inside the café it was just the two of us. Our gum-popping waitress, Madge, had on her usual too-tight brown uniform with a stained apron over the front. On my first visit to this café, I had learned to never look at Madge as she walked away. Let's just say she wore underwear of the type that not even a skinny woman could be comfortable in. And Madge was far from thin, no matter how small a uniform she jammed herself into every day.

The Diner was one of those toss-backs to the 1950s and early 1960s, with phony decorations and everything in red and black checks, including the tile on the floor and the booths. It just glared pretend memories. I didn't need to pretend to have memories – I had enough real ones of my own.

The minute we had dropped into a booth, I had used Patty's cell phone to call the third member of our superhero trio. Screamer, a guy who could take the thoughts out of one person's mind and let another person see them. He also could roam around inside a person's head on touch, and make them see things they didn't want to see. He got his nickname from making a mass-murderer scream so loud that the murderer damaged his vocal cords and had to write down where he had buried ten different bodies. Screamer often worked with the Las Vegas police and casino owners.

I just had a gut feeling that we were going to need him.

When I had told Screamer that Patty and I had an important case, he had said. "At The Diner?"

"Yup," I had said.

"Be there in ten minutes." Not even one complaint about it being Christmas Eve.

For over five cases now, since the great Ghost Slots case, we had used The Diner as a meeting place. It was like a second home for all three of us in Vegas.

No one was on The Diner's five slots tonight, which for some reason made me feel a little better about humanity in general. Usually the elderly played those slots at all times of the day or night, pumping away their retirement savings simply because they had nothing better to do with their time. Hitting a small jackpot gave them a moment of excitement, a feeling of youth for a fleeting second before the bell stopped and the machine asked for another dollar.

At least tonight, on this one special night, they had something else to do for a few hours. Chances are some of them would be back tomorrow.

Patty and I decided to split a chocolate milkshake, since the milkshakes here were large enough to send a normal person into a diabetic coma. Patty had had dinner at the Mirage earlier with her father, and my wonderful turkey and gravy from the buffet was still keeping me satisfied. Madge had just brought the shake when Screamer came in and dropped into the booth beside Patty.

Screamer's real name was Toledo Moss, and he looked like any other tourist you would see walking the Strip, with his short cut brown hair, his dark glasses, his loud Hawaiian shirt, Bermuda shorts, and sandals.

Screamer had lived in Vegas his entire life and knew exactly how to blend in. No one looking at any of us sitting in that booth would think we were three superheroes, fighting to help the weak, and this time bring luck back to the planet.

"I'm hearing rumors that something big is going on," Screamer said turning back to face me after he asked Madge for his own chocolate shake.

"Laverne is missing," Patty said.

Screamer snorted, just as I had done, then laughed. I'm glad I wasn't the only one who snorted at the news.

"Stan told us a few minutes before I called you," I said. "She's been missing for two and a half hours now."

Screamer stared at me, then glanced at Patty to see her serious face before turning back to face me across the booth. "Is luck missing as well?"

I nodded. "Completely, from the entire world, from what Stan said."

Screamer opened his mouth, then closed it, clearly stunned.

We all sat there for a long minute, just thinking, until finally Screamer said, "I can't imagine the world without luck."

I shrugged. "Since I'm a poker player and don't believe in luck, I can imagine it just fine. Everything will just continue to happen as it statistically should."

Screamer again started to say something, then smiled and stared right at me. "Poker Boy, I can tell you have a plan."

"Read me like a book," I said, smiling back. "First off, we need to figure out who would get the most out of Lady Luck, and all luck for that matter, being gone. Who would have the power to trick or trap Laverne and hold her, and gain by doing so?"

"Not many, I would guess," Patty said.

"That's what we need to find out," I said.

Patty and Screamer both nodded so I went on. "Second, we need to find out statistically what the chances are for different causes of Laverne's vanishing. Since luck is no longer with us, only numbers will dictate what happened – or will happen – to her."

"And how are we going to do that?" Screamer asked.

"Oh, don't tell me," Patty said, staring at me, looking disgusted.

I didn't blame her. Just the idea had me feeling a little nauseous, but I could see no choice. "The Bookkeeper."

"Oh, no chance," Screamer said, shaking his head from side to side. "I'd rather crawl around in a mass murderer's head than go into that house again."

"I'll do it," I said, sounding a lot more sure of myself than I actually did. The Bookkeeper was the most brilliant statistician in history, and a superhero over in the mathematics world of gods. He had been around and working for the Gods for centuries. However, he looked very much like a rat, and his house smelled so bad that last time I went in there I had to stand in a shower for an hour to even pretend to get the smell off of me.

"Good," Screamer said. "I'll start asking around about who had it out for Laverne, who was feuding with her, that sort of thing."

"I'll go with you," Patty said to me, "but I'm changing into old clothes first."

"Thanks," I said. "We're a long-shot on solving this."

"Not as long a shot as you might think," Screamer said. "The three of us are a pretty powerful team."

I could only nod at that, but I still didn't believe we had much of a chance. We were only lowly superheroes. Lady Luck was one of the top gods of all gods. And without luck, who knew what would happen.

Screamer stood and tossed a five on the table to pay for

the milkshake Madge hadn't delivered yet. "I'll get going, see what I can dig up, meet you two back here? How long?"

"Three hours," I said. "We'll need time for showers."

"Good luck out there." He turned and headed for the door.

Patty and I sat, just enjoying each other's company as we finished our milkshake and part of Screamer's. Neither of us was in a real hurry to wade into that smell that filled the Book-keeper's home.

CHAPTER THREE

Patty changed clothes while I waited in the car outside of her condo, not really wanting to chance going upstairs and getting distracted. Twenty minutes later, we pulled up in front of the dark house belonging to The Bookkeeper.

It was a standard, suburban house in a pretty standard subdivision. Only unlike the others along the street, his house had no landscaping at all, just weeds and covered-over windows. The house had tall fences on both sides, built by the neighbors to shut off the look of the house from the rest of the homes along the silent street. Christmas decorations lit up most of the homes, looking odd in the desert climate. Only The Bookkeeper's house had no decorations, and clearly hadn't been painted in decades.

I left my hat and coat in the car, not wanting to get my superhero costume smelling so much I couldn't wear it again. I had other black coats and other hats that worked just as well as a superhero costume, but they were back in Oregon in my double-wide trailer near the casino. Luckily I had left a few changes of regular clothes, including another pair of shoes, in Patty's apartment a month or so back, so I could change everything but my coat and hat after we were finished here.

About halfway up the sidewalk on this warm Christmas Eve, the smell started to hit us, and by the time we were standing at the door, my eyes were watering.

Let me try to describe this smell. Imagine a full garbage can behind a fish restaurant sitting in the sun for a few days, then combine that with a dirty cat box that hadn't been changed for a month, and mix in a full latrine stench.

Yeah, bad didn't begin to describe it.

"You don't need to do this," I said to Patty, trying to cover my nose with my arm but failing miserably.

"I have a hunch this is going to need us both," Patty said, blinking hard and clearly trying to not choke.

I had learned while working with Patty that her "hunches" were part of her super power as Front Desk Girl. It was her ability to foresee problems for guests in hotels before they actually happened. I never doubted her hunches, and they had always been right so far.

I banged on the door, then rang the doorbell. We both stepped back, trying to get away from the smell a little and waited.

Nothing.

I banged on the door again, then shouted, "Bookkeeper, it's Poker Boy. I need to talk to you!"

Nothing.

The super ability that kept me out of bad situations and bad poker hands was going off like a large gong in my head. Something was very wrong here, and my warning wanted me to avoid it. I often ignored that warning, especially in rescue situations.

I glanced at Patty. "You feeling it?"

She nodded.

Suddenly, a car pulled up behind Patty's car and Screamer climbed out. There was no reason for him to be here except to warn us about something or tell us that Laverne had been found. I was hoping for the latter, but my senses were telling me that wasn't the case.

We went down the driveway to meet him, trying to put some distance between us and the smell radiating out of that house.

"Glad I caught you," Screamer said. "You could be walking into a trap. It's The Bookkeeper who has had a problem with Lady Luck lately."

"You're kidding," I said. "He's no more than a superhero like we are. Why would he go up against Lady Luck herself?"

"He's crazy," Patty said, waving her hand in front of her nose to make her point, as if any of us could forget the smell the Bookkeeper lived in.

"He's been claiming that he can prove that luck is not

needed in the universe," Screamer said, "that it is a man-made assumption to explain statistical occurrences."

"If he actually proved that, then Lady Luck would vanish," Patty said.

"And The Bookkeeper would be in charge," I said, glancing at the dark, ugly, smelling house behind us. "We need to get in there and find out what is really going on."

I went back to Patty's car and got my hat and coat and put them on. Smell or not, I was going to need the power. Patty grabbed a flashlight out of her glove box, then the three of us headed up the driveway toward the front door, fighting our way into the waves of smell.

At the front door, Patty put her hand on the door handle and I could hear the lock click.

It seemed that another power that Front Desk Girl had was helping people into their rooms after they'd locked themselves out. I just figured that power would be in making a new key, but I had learned a few cases back that it extended to opening just about anything that was locked.

"I'm going to be ready to shift us out of time," I said as I took Patty's hand. "Screamer, stay close."

He nodded. I had discovered during the problems with the Ghost Slots that an extension of my ability to stop and analyze a poker hand extended to taking myself out of time, or basically freezing time around me. Stan had first showed me that trick, but it wasn't until I was with Patty that I had learned how to do it myself. On our last adventure, I had saved the three of us from getting killed by a huge wall of water washing down a dry gulch as we looked for an ancient burial ground of the Silicon Suckers. I just stopped time and the three of us moved out of the way of the water.

I just hoped that if something happened here I could do it again quickly.

It was just too bad that none of the three of us had an odor-repelling super power.

I led the way as we waded into the thick smell of the dark living room. The air got warmer, which made the smell even worse, if that was possible. The farther we got into the room, the more worried about this I felt.

The living room was piled high with rotting boxes of who-knew-what kind of trash. A path wound its way through the boxes toward the hallway and the back room where The Bookkeeper kept his computer set up with a small bed tucked in one corner.

In the faint light of the flashlight that Patty held, I could see littered remains of hundreds of different meals, mostly T.V. dinners, some still covered with black flies. Disgusting didn't begin to describe it.

Behind me Patty coughed softly and Screamer just said "Oh, man."

The house was a standard ranch house, with three bedrooms and a bath down a hallway off of the living room. I knew, from the last time I had been here, that The Bookkeeper had set up his computer in the first bedroom on the right, across from a bathroom that smelled like the toilet had been used and used and not flushed in five years.

A faint light came from the computer room, and the humming sounds of powerful computers working filled the hallway.

Every sense in my body was telling me to turn and get out of here, to lay down this hand and just go to the next one. But sometimes in a hand you are what is called "pot committed," and in this instance, we were committed to finding out what was happening in that small bedroom, no matter how much I really didn't want to know.

I eased into the room where The Bookkeeper sat hunched over a keyboard, his fingers flying faster over the keys than I thought humanly possible.

"Bookkeeper," I said. "It's Poker Boy."

"I was wrong," he said, not stopping. "I'm sure I was wrong. I just have to prove it."

"Wrong about what?" I asked, stepping far enough into the small room that Patty and Screamer could move into the door behind me. In my mind I extended an area around the three of us and held that image just in case I needed to shift us out of time very, very quickly. I had no idea what The Book-keeper would do next, but I wanted to be ready for anything.

"About luck," he said. "I have to prove she exists very quickly, before everything starts to unravel."

He pointed to his right between keystrokes; then, without missing a beat, kept typing.

"Oh, my," Patty said from behind me, flashing her light to the right where The Bookkeeper had pointed. In the beam of light, unseen in the darkness of the room, was Lady Luck.

Actually, it was just a faint, shimmering image of Lady Luck, frozen in mid-sentence. The beam from Patty's flashlight went right through her.

Even like that, Lady Luck still scared hell out of me.

"She's slowly vanishing," Screamer said.

CHAPTER FOUR

"I used twelve of the world's most powerful computers, linked up, to prove that luck did not exist," The Bookkeeper said, never looking up, never stopping his work. "And she ended up here, frozen in a moment, slowly fading. I had no intention of killing Lady Luck. I was just trying to prove a point."

"And if she vanishes completely?" Patty asked.

"Then slowly the rest of the world starts to do the same. Everything as we know it will slowly unravel."

"Why?" I asked.

"I don't know," The Bookkeeper said. "But that's what the computers tell me will happen if Luck dies."

"And now you're trying to do what exactly?" I asked.

"Prove that luck, Lady Luck does exist," he said.

I glanced back at Patty and Screamer. Patty's wonderful

eyes were wider than normal which let me know she was both afraid and very worried. Screamer just looked intent, staring at Lady Luck.

Prove that luck existed. How could anyone do that?

I concentrated for an instant and took all three of us out of time, leaving The Bookkeeper in mid-stoke of the keyboard. We needed to talk and not have him hear us. I could hold all three of us in a bubble out of time for about a minute.

"Do you actually think The Bookkeeper's calculations brought Laverne here?" Patty asked.

"I have no doubt of that," Screamer said.

"Neither do I," I said. "Statistics are one of the greatest forces in the world, governing everything in every detail of life as we know it. I'm sure that power could do this, especially to Lady Luck, and she wouldn't even know what hit her. I've seen it a million times in poker hand after poker hand. Statistics win out over luck."

"I agree," Screamer said. "And clearly The Bookkeeper here is a master of statistics."

"And now he's trying to undo what he has done," Patty said.

I started to agree, but then one of my special powers kicked in. It was a power that sort of had a faint "ding" that signaled to my mind that it was in use. A "ding" that I had missed something that was important to the situation. When I heard that "ding" in my mind, I always stopped and went back over what had just happened. The power had saved me a lot of money on the poker tables.

It took me a moment, because I was also holding the bubble of the three of us out of time, but then I realized what I had missed. The Bookkeeper was not in charge of statistics, was not the master of them at all. He was only a lowly superhero like we were. He had a boss just like the rest of us.

I dropped us back to real time. "Bookkeeper, who is your boss?"

"A guy named Harold. Haven't seen him in a few hundred years."

"We'll be right back," I said, then nodded to Screamer and Patty that we should head outside.

The Bookkeeper didn't even slow down in the slightest.

The moment we were back outside into the warm Christmas Eve night, I shouted into the air, "Stan!"

He appeared near Patty's car and then motioned for us to stop about five feet away, wrinkling his nose. "Wow, do you three smell. What do you need?"

"Who is Harold? And who is Harold's boss?"

Stan frowned. "Harold is the God of Mathematics. He and the God of Physics, Merle, and the God of Chemistry, Bettie, hang around together and pretty much look down their noses at all the Gambling Gods and even the other science gods. They pretty much run their own area. I don't know if they actually report in to anyone these days. Why?"

"We found Laverne," I said, nodding to the dark house. "Is there any bad blood between them and Laverne?"

"You found her!" Stan said.

"Hang on," I said, stopping Stan from rushing into the

house. "We don't really know what's going on yet and I think we had better find out before doing anything. So any bad blood between Laverne and any of the science gods?"

Stan shook his head, "None that I know of."

A moment later a heavy-set man wearing a three-piece suit appeared beside Stan. He had an unlit cigar in one hand. He glanced around and then wrinkled his nose. "The Bookkeeper's place I assume?"

Stan nodded.

Patty, Screamer, and I said nothing. It wasn't often that the god who was second in command to Laverne just appeared in front of you. Burt scared me, but not half as bad as Laverne did.

"Any fights lately between Laverne and the science geeks?" Stan asked.

"Nothing that I know of," Burt said. "Why?"

"Then we need them here," I said, "and maybe the god in charge of humanities or human nature as well."

Burt stared at me like I was a fly on a steak he was about to eat. I stood my ground, even though every sense in my body wanted me to just cower away.

"Why?" he demanded.

I quickly told him what we had found in there, and what The Bookkeeper had done and was now trying to undo. I finished with "He needs help, and it isn't the kind of help any of us can give him. In fact, if we try anything, we might end up completely killing Laverne."

"Poker Boy is right," Screamer said. "The Bookkeeper

might be able to prove that luck doesn't exist, but proving luck exists is another matter."

I couldn't have said it better myself, so I said nothing more.

Burt stared at Screamer, then at me, then at Patty. A moment later we were all standing in a very large, very plush library office, with books that went up all four walls to a very high ceiling. As far as I could see in all directions, it was library walls and books. There had to be millions of books in here. Just the thought of that gave me a headache. I got a lot of headaches back in my college days.

A crackling fire filled a large stone fireplace on one wall, and three overstuffed leather chairs circled the fireplace. Clearly this was where Harold, Merle, and Bettie spent a lot of time.

At the moment all three were standing, as if informed we were coming.

"What do we owe this Christmas Eve visit to?" asked a man with a heavy cardigan sweater and an unlit pipe in his hand. Another man with thick round glasses and a bald head stood beside him, and Bettie stood slightly off to one side looking the perfect image of an old school teacher from the Wild West.

"Thank you for seeing us, Harold," Burt said.

"What is that odor?" Bettie said, waving her hand in front of her nose. Then the God of Chemistry waved her hand at me and Screamer and Patty and the foul stench of The Book-keeper's house vanished.

I wanted to thank her, but instead kept silent as Burt quickly explained what one of their lowly superheroes had done to Lady Luck.

"The Bookkeeper did that?" Harold said, smiling to himself. "I am impressed."

"That explains the smell," Bettie said, nodding to us. "You went to see him, didn't you?"

"It would be impressive," Burt said, "Except that Laverne is trapped by his equations, and slowly fading from existence."

"And The Bookkeeper is working as fast as he can to prove that luck *does* exist to bring her back," I said. "But he needs help."

Harold smiled and nodded. "I can imagine he would at that. He would make the equations far, far harder than they would need to be."

Merle nodded. "It's like a quantum physics problem, actually. The Bookkeeper might have been able to prove that in perfect conditions, statistics prove that luck does not exist. That would have been enough to trap Laverne without warning. But luck is governed and influenced by the observer. And thus the observer changes the equation by simply observing it. Simple, actually."

I didn't think it was so simple, but clearly Harold and Bettie understood him. Burt, Stan, and the three of us were just nodding, as if we actually understood any of that.

"Can you help The Bookkeeper reverse what he has done to Laverne?" Burt asked.

Harold nodded and turned to me and Patty and Screamer.

"Since the three of you have been in that house once tonight, I assume you can go back in. Correct?"

We all nodded.

"Tell The Bookkeeper I told him to add into his equation the factor of an observer. That should break what is holding Laverne. But tell him to go slowly. Very slowly."

Burt nodded. "Thanks. I'm sure Laverne will stop by to thank you as well."

CHAPTER FIVE

An instant later we were back out in front of The Bookkeeper's home.

I glanced at Stan and Burt, then turned to Patty and Screamer. "No need for the two of you to go in there again."

The moment I said that, I knew that I was wrong.

Patty shook her head and Screamer looked worried.

"I think we all need to do this," Patty said.

Burt and Stan both nodded. "Harold told all three of you to do it, so it's going to take the three of you for some strange reason.

I couldn't argue with my two bosses, and my little voice, the one that controlled most of my actions, both at a poker table and away from it, was now happy again.

Bracing ourselves once more against the smell, which is

just damned impossible to do, we fought our way upstream through the front room and back to where The Bookkeeper pounded the keys.

Laverne looked very, very faint.

My little voice told me that I needed to get us all close together and be ready to get us out of real time very quickly. Harold had said that what I was to tell The Bookkeeper would break the equations holding Laverne. I didn't like the sounds of the word "break" at all.

"Bookkeeper," I said when Screamer and Patty were in position beside me, "we went to see Harold."

The Bookkeeper just kept working, his fingers pounding the keyboard, the screens in front of him flashing numbers and calculations faster than I could follow, even if I knew what I was looking at.

"Harold said to add in the factor of an observer into your equation."

"Sure he did, sure," The Bookkeeper said.

Laverne seemed to fade a little more and The Bookkeeper just kept working.

I clicked us out of time and turned to Screamer. "He doesn't believe me, he's so trapped and scared."

"I can show him the image of Harold and Merle and Bettie," Screamer said.

"Patty, can you calm him down?" I asked. I knew that another of Patty's special abilities is to get a person to calm down when they are very, very upset.

"I can," Patty said. She looked worried still.

"What are you thinking?" I asked, staring as best I could in the dim light into her dark brown eyes.

"I'm worried about what's going to happen when the spell holding one of the most powerful women in all of time breaks."

"Yeah, me too," I said. "And I don't think The Bookkeeper, to rescue Laverne, can go slowly. I don't think there's enough time."

Screamer nodded that he too had thought about that.

Patty looked at me. "If he can't do it slowly, you need to surround The Bookkeeper as well the moment he types in the equation that will break the hold on Laverne."

I nodded. "The timing on this is going to be critical. Screamer, you be touching The Bookkeeper and Patty and I will be touching you, so we know the instant we need to move."

"Got it," he said.

I wanted to take a deep breath and say, "Let's do it." But a deep breath of this air might knock me out, so instead I just nodded and released us back into real time.

As a unit we stepped over behind The Bookkeeper. I held Patty's hand and then touched Screamer's shoulder, keeping my mind focused on an area around the four of us.

When Patty touched Screamer an instant later, I got a sense of her thoughts, her worries. They were the same as mine. And Screamer's. We were all scared to death.

Screamer reached forward and touched the back of The

Bookkeeper's shoulder. All I could feel at that point was massive panic and fear.

Patty quickly calmed him down, and me and Screamer as well with a simple thought.

"I see, I see, I understand," The Bookkeeper said, nodding as Screamer transferred the images from the vast library into his head.

"But I can't go slowly."

He stopped and turned to us, but because we were all touching Screamer, we all knew exactly what he meant. Laverne was too far gone. Going slowly was not an option, and we all knew it because we were all linked.

So Screamer put in The Bookkeeper's head what we planned on doing, and The Bookkeeper nodded. "Only chance we have."

He turned back to his keyboard, paused only for a second, then began quickly typing again.

In the corner Laverne started to firm up, slowly, her image not so faint.

The Bookkeeper kept pounding the keys.

Patty kept us all calm.

Screamer kept the communication links opened.

And I stood ready to snap us out of time and away from any danger.

"That should do it," The Bookkeeper said, pounding one finger on the enter key.

<u>Now!</u>

The thought from Screamer was like a shout in my head.

I snapped us out of time a tiny fraction of a second before the explosion started to tear through the house and all space around us.

Close. Too damned close.

Screamer grabbed The Bookkeeper and yanked his small frame out of the chair, carrying him as we all turned for the door.

"Stay near me," I said, working to hold the bubble around all four of us as we worked our way toward the front door. Patty kept her hand in mine, sending as much strength and energy into me as she could to help me hold the field as long as I could.

Outside, on the driveway, Stan and Burt were standing frozen, clearly waiting for us to come out, not realizing I had taken us out of time. The four of us moved down the driveway toward them, and I surrounded them as well with my field, barely holding it.

"Stan," I said, the moment he and Burt were inside the bubble and could see us, "I need help holding this time bubble."

Instantly Stan took over and I almost slumped to the ground with the release. I was still creating the bubble, but Stan was powering it.

"I have a hunch we need to be a little farther away than this," Screamer said.

"I agree," The Bookkeeper said, his breath worse than the smell of his house.

"No need to worry," Burt said. "Stan can you hold this for another few seconds?"

"No problem," Stan said.

Burt closed his eyes and focused for a moment, then nodded and opened them. "It's been a while since I needed to do that."

"What?" Patty asked.

"I put a force field cone around the house, so that any explosion will be focused upward about five hundred feet. We're outside that cone, so it's safe to let us go."

Stan nodded to me and I released us all back into real time.

The explosion was deafening as The Bookkeeper's house just flat vanished into a dust cloud that went straight up.

A very smelly dust cloud. The neighbors, and much of Las Vegas, were not going to be happy with that smell.

Out of the dust cloud and force field that Burt had raised walked Laverne. She was totally nude, since the explosion had vaporized her clothes. And she looked really pissed off.

"Someone want to explain to me just what the hell is going on?"

Burt sort of pointed at Laverne's midsection and at that moment Laverne noticed she was nude. I had to admit, for such an ancient god, she kept in pretty good shape.

Clothes appeared on her and she didn't blink, keeping her stare on Burt. Clearly they were communicating in a way I didn't want to think about.

After a moment, she turned on The Bookkeeper. But

before she could do anything to him, Harold appeared beside the smelly man and nodded. "Glad to see you well, Laverne. I'll take care of The Bookkeeper. Very sorry for the bother."

And then they were gone.

Laverne took a deep breath, then coughed. Into the air she shouted "Bettie, can you do something about this smell?"

A moment later the air around us smelled like a spring meadow. Even my jacket and hat smelled like a freshly mowed lawn.

Up and down the street people were coming out to stare at the giant hole where The Bookkeeper's house used to be. No doubt, the property values in the neighborhood had just taken a huge jump, but I was going to be real curious to know how the police explained this one to the press.

Laverne turned to the three of us, and stared first at me.

I wanted to melt right there into the driveway, but instead stood my ground and stared back at her, giving her my best poker face. I couldn't talk, but I could stare just fine.

"It seems," she said after a very, very long moment, "that I once again owe you three a thank you."

"It's just our job," Patty said, smiling.

"Well," Laverne said, "thank you for doing your job so well, and for saving me. I hope you have a great holiday. You all three deserve some time off."

With that, she and Burt vanished.

Stan turned to us and just smiled. "Nice job, guys." Then he too vanished.

Screamer clapped his hands together and laughed. "Damned if we didn't do it again."

I was still too stunned to say anything. Seems face-to-face meetings with Lady Luck just did that to me.

"There's a large steak waiting for me down at the MGM Grand," Screamer said. "You two want to join me?"

Patty put her arm around my waist and smiled. "I think we'll take a rain check on that."

Two hours later, after a long, long shower with far too much use of soap between us, and a long, wonderful time in bed, I stared at the beautiful women lying next to me.

"What are you thinking?" she asked.

I just leaned in and kissed her as a response.

Right at that moment all was well in the world. There was no doubt that luck still existed.

And that I was the luckiest man alive.

The Fun Starts Here

Just Turn The Page...

SNEAK PEEK

Being Dead (The First Year)

CHAPTER ONE

Dying on a first date sucks.

Dying on a blind date sucks even worse.

Especially when your date dies with you. And then goes off through some tunnel of light into the next life or something, leaving you sitting alone, dead, in a dark alley, waiting for your own tunnel of light.

Hands down, the worst ending to any date in recorded history.

The alley we had been forced to go into was blacker than the inside of a latrine, and seeing how it smelled, I would have not been surprised to be in a latrine, but I knew I wasn't since it seemed that being dead meant I could see just fine in the dark.

And smell just fine as well. Holy crap. The nearby Chinese restaurant garbage smelled like my fridge after six days of feeling sorry for myself and laying on the couch and eating take-out without taking out the uneaten food in the original cartons. And no telling how many homeless and drunks had actually used this alley for a bathroom.

I was sitting on a big green dumpster owned by a nearby office, so thankfully it didn't have the odor of the other dumpsters coming up between my legs.

The scum with the greasy black hair and dirty ski parka that had killed us was going through my date's pockets as I sat and watched.

The guy looked skinny and no doubt drug-addicted. His motions were jerky, his eyes darting around him like a rat trying to find a way out of a maze.

My blind date, dear old Handsome Bob, as I had started to think of him for the full thirty minutes I had known him, had caused this mess by thinking he could be a macho asshole or something.

The scum with the greasy black hair had approached us on the sidewalk and Bob had shaken his head and said, "Not now."

We were headed down the street to a nice Italian restaurant that served the best red wine and bread plate this side of New York. And that was going some for the Old Towne section of Boise, Idaho.

Bob was dressed in a clearly expensive silk suit and no tie, while I didn't look so cheap myself. For the date I had put on dark slacks, a white silk blouse with pearls around my neck, and a thin see-through sweater. No bra because I wanted my date to get an occasional peek at what might be offered after dinner if things went right.

Sitting dead in an alley sure wasn't my idea of things going right.

The greasy jerk had pulled out a gun, his hands shaking. Dear old dead Handsome Bob had said, "You don't want to do that."

Bless him.

Clearly the druggie did want to do exactly what he was doing, but I didn't say that. I was busy ramping up one of my super powers.

You see, before I was so suddenly cut down, I had worked as a superhero in the housing and hotel industry. Over the last century I had worked both front desks of hotels and sold real estate. At the moment I was on the real estate side, trying to help out in the booming Boise real estate market.

Amazing the kind of crap that goes on in real estate when big money is involved.

I hit greasy-hair with a full dose of my calming power. The guy was so high on drugs my power actually didn't do anything but make him stop shaking so hard.

He pointed to the dark alley with the gun. "Get in there and then dig out your money."

"And if we say no?" Handsome Bob asked the guy.

Since Bob was almost a foot taller than the greasy-haired druggie, I suppose Bob thought he could bully the situation a little.

Bless dear old now-dead stupid Bob.

I hit the guy with another dose of calming power. I had enough power on a normal day to stop a shouting, irate, pissed-off hotel customer at a front desk and make them smile.

The guy with the gun got calmer, but his pea brain was still set on robbing us. At least I got him to not shoot us right there on the sidewalk because of Handsome Bob's stupidity.

"Let's just give him our stuff and he will let us go," I said to Bob.

"Smart woman," the guy said, smiling and showing a mouthful of rotted teeth.

Actually, I had planned that when we got into the alley I would simply jump us away from this nut and then figure out something to tell dear old Bob.

Bob didn't know I was a one-hundred-year-old superhero and could just teleport anywhere I wanted. Not something you tell someone before a first blind date. Men tended to have sexual problems when they realized the woman they were with was over a hundred.

Bob nodded to me and we walked the twenty steps into the alley, Bob pushing me slightly ahead of him.

Then, as we stopped and turned at just about the point where the rotted Chinese food odor got the worst, Bob went to lunge at the guy.

Handsome Bob went to really, really stupid Bob very quickly.

I was so surprised Bob would do something that idiotic, I didn't react fast enough to jump us out of there.

The guy fired, hitting Bob in the arm.

The bullet went through Bob's flesh and hit me square between the eyes.

Now that was a shocker, let me tell you.

One moment I am standing alive in the alley and the next I am a ghost sitting on a smelly dumpster watching dear old Handsome Bob hold his arm and swear.

The greasy-haired guy was now twitching again. He stared at my body lying there in the alley, clearly getting my wonderful blouse and sweater all stained up with my own blood.

Then he looked at Bob, who was also staring at me, holding his wounded arm and looking sick to his stomach.

Then the guy did what any self-respecting murderer would do. He shot Bob.

Bob slumped to the ground and the guy fired one more shot into Bob's head.

A moment later I watched Bob's ghost stand up, look around, then look up and float off into a white light.

"Nice meeting you jerk-face," I shouted after Bob.

I was pretty sure he didn't hear me.

As I said, the worst ending to a blind date ever.

Chapter Two

The druggie who had killed me and my blind date started through Bob's pockets. The druggie pulled out a money clip and then took Bob's watch. Then he rolled Bob over slightly and took out his wallet.

He pulled out a single-package condom and tossed it aside.

I just shook my head. "Damn, Bob, only one? Where was the confidence? If you had come back to my place, you would have needed at least three just to make it to breakfast."

The greasy murderer clearly didn't hear me. And I had a hunch dead Bob didn't either.

I glanced around. I was still the only ghost in the alley.

Where was my greeting party?

I figured I had become a Ghost Agent, which was why I hadn't gotten the beam-of-light ride. I had never met a Ghost

Agent, but I had heard from my best friend Patty that she and her boyfriend, Poker Boy, had worked with some Ghost Agents just lately to save the world. Seems Patty and her boyfriend were always saving the world, which I must admit I appreciated.

The guy stood and stepped toward my body.

"Hey, not so fast there, jerk-face," I said, jumping down from the dumpster and brushing off my pants.

The greasy-haired slime-ball picked up my clutch purse and went through it. That I didn't much care about. I had a few hundred in there and that was that.

But then he looked around at the mouth of the alley and then looked back at me with that look I had seen scum like him get. Ghost or no ghost, he wasn't touching me, even if I did have a hole in the middle of my forehead.

This night had gone bad enough as it was.

The guy kneeled down beside my body and I took two quick steps at the guy and went to kick him clear across the alley.

Foot went right through him. Charlie Brown would have been proud of my form, though. I didn't end up on my back.

However, when my foot went through the guy, I got to read all of his thoughts.

All of what he was about to do to me.

So I closed my eyes and went inside the scum. Now I knew for a fact I was in a cesspool, swimming in the shit that this guy called thoughts. If I got out of here I would need about ten showers.

If ghosts took showers.

As he reached for my right breast, I shouted at the top of my lungs, "No!"

And trust me, I can be loud.

Just ask anyone who sat beside me at a Broncos' football game.

And I was inside the guy when I shouted.

Slime-bucket grabbed his head and rolled over backward, the intense pain striking everywhere.

As he rolled away, I managed to stand my ground and get out of his body. I shook myself, wishing I could forget the memories of what I had just seen in his mind.

It would take twenty showers before I would feel clean again.

The guy was holding his head and screaming and rolling on the ground. Blood was coming out of his ears.

Both ears.

"Wow, what did you do to him?" a voice behind me asked.

I turned around to see a handsome couple standing to one side looking shocked. Both were about my height of five-ten, both wore jeans, expensive shirts, and tennis shoes.

"The pervert was about to get his jollies on my dead body, so I climbed inside his head and shouted as loud as I could."

Both of them laughed.

Then the woman stepped forward. "I'm Jewel and this is Tommy. We came to help get you used to being a ghost, but guess you are doing just fine."

I shook both their hands, happy as hell I had company.

"I'm Marble Grant. And got a hunch I'm going to need a lot of help."

"Someone close to you?" Tommy asked, pointing at Handsome Bob.

"Knew him for thirty minutes," I said. "Blind date. But I had planned on getting much closer to him after dinner, if you get my drift."

Jewel laughed and Tommy actually blushed a little, which I loved. I had a feeling I was going to like these two.

"I suppose you two are Ghost Agents. Right?"

Both of them looked shocked.

"I was a superhero in the hospitality and real estate side of the world," I said. "Any chance you two know Patty Ledgerwood and Poker Boy?"

"We do," Jewel said.

"You know," I said, "I'm damn hungry and I assume there is a way ghosts eat, so any chance we could get out of this smell and grab a bite and you guys call Patty and have her meet us. I would kind of like to tell her about my sudden death myself, since she has been my best friend for a hundred years now, give or take."

Both of them just nodded.

"Anything we need to do with that guy?" I asked, looking down at the scum who had killed me and Handsome Bob before I had the chance to find out if the handsome part went all the way to Bob's southern regions.

Greasy hair was still rolling on the dirty concrete, holding his ears and screaming. He was losing a lot of blood through his fingers. I clearly had done some damage.

"I think he's finished," Tommy said, laughing.

"Yeah," Jewel said. "Got to remember that trick."

With that we jumped to a place I knew well and loved, the Golden Nugget Buffet in downtown Las Vegas.

Now I knew I was really going to like these two.

Chapter Three

The Golden Nugget Buffet had been decorated in all warm brown cloth and polished brass. Plants ringed the outside of the side part of the dining room nearest the escalator and the tables were solid, as were the chairs.

My hand went right through a chair as I tried to pull it out and Jewel did it for me.

"You'll learn how to actually move some physical matter, but you don't want to do that too often because people start to get spooked."

"I'll bet," I said.

Tommy jumped away to find Patty, and Jewel led me up to the wonderful smelling food. The images from the murderer's head were slowly fading, something I was very grateful for.

"Be careful to not run into anyone," Jewel said, indicating the six people around the large buffet area. "You end up reading their thoughts."

"Yeah, learned that with the guy who shot me," I said.

Jewel showed me how to pick up a plate, which was actually just the ghost component of the plate, and how to take food from the buffet.

In five minutes of filling a ghost plate with ghost food, I managed to not run into anyone alive, which sort of felt like a victory. I called it the dance of the living. A living person came toward me, I stepped sideways and went around them.

Jewel did the same, seemingly without noticing.

Back at the table, I bit into a piece of prime rib and damn near had an orgasm right there at the table.

Jewel just smiled as I moaned and kept on eating the fantastic tasting food.

"I remember the food being good here," I said after a few bites, "but never this good."

"Everything is better when you are a ghost," Jewel said. "Food tastes better, emotions are more powerful, and the travel and living is easier."

"Sex?" I asked.

"As the joke goes," Jewel said, smiling, "it's to die for."

"Oh, no," I said. "I had enough trouble controlling myself when I was alive."

Jewel just laughed and at that moment Tommy appeared.

"Patty is in Poker Boy's office," Tommy said. "Let's just

grab some food and jump there. She's expecting us but doesn't know why yet."

It dawned on me why Patty couldn't jump here. She was still alive. Anyone in the restaurant would see her arrive and then talk to no one. Not a good idea.

Tommy headed for the buffet. I really needed to pee, but instead I kept eating as we waited for him. Damn, the food was so good. I was going to be lucky to not gain a ton of weight now that I had died. I needed to remember to ask Jewel and Tommy how they stayed so thin.

After Tommy came back with a full plate of food, he jumped the three of us and our food and drink to what I assumed was Poker Boy's office, although I had never been there.

In fact, the place was like a legend.

But I had heard it was something special and I had heard right. The office wasn't really an office. It was more like a tile platform floating in the air a thousand feet over the Strip.

All four walls were freaking clear glass with a wood railing about waist high all the way around.

Without that railing, I would have been so afraid of falling off that slick checkered tile floor, I would have been clinging to the furniture and screaming like a ten-year-old girl not wanting to go see her uncle.

And I was dead, so pretty certain the fall wouldn't kill me again.

Still, scary damn place and now I really had to pee.

I made my heart stop racing and looked around.

In the very center of the room was this huge 1950s style diner booth, with a scarred tabletop and red vinyl booth seats on three sides. The thing was big enough to hold ten people if the people really liked each other.

There were half-a-dozen chairs around the room that could be pulled up to the open end of the booth I suppose, but three of them just sat facing out over the incredible view of the city.

And wow, what a view. I had always loved the lights of Las Vegas. Just never seen them from the air like this before.

"Marble," Patty said as we appeared. "Tommy said you needed to talk with me. Everything all right? You could have just called you know?"

"Not sure I knew how exactly," I said, smiling at my best friend.

Jewel laughed as she set her food and mine on the booth table.

Patty was wearing her MGM Grand Front Desk uniform of dark slacks, tan blouse and a lighter tan vest. She had her long hair pulled back and was as stunning as ever.

Patty frowned, something I had rarely seen her do in a century.

I glanced at my food on the booth table, then turned back to my friend. "Got myself killed while on a blind date about thirty minutes ago."

Patty's eyes went totally round. "Are you all right?"

"Pretty sure I'm dead," I said, laughing. I pointed to my forehead. "Bullet right there did the trick."

Patty looked like she was about to cry.

"Can I hug her?" I asked, glancing back at Jewel.

"She's a superhero," Jewel said, "and she can see you, so sure, don't know why not?"

I stepped toward Patty and she hugged me so hard, I wasn't sure I would be able to breathe.

And I hugged her back.

I guess, for the first time, it was sinking in that I had really died.

I was still here but I was dead.

That just sucked.

Except for the part about the food tasting so much better.

Finish Reading

Being Dead (The First Year): A Marble Grant Novel

Get More Marble Grant

Hear From Dean

Want More From Dean?

For Dean Wesley Smith's newsletter
go to deanwesleysmith.com.

Get the latest news and releases from all of WMG's authors
and lines, including Kristine Grayson, Kris Nelscott,
Pulphouse Magazine, and so much more…

To sign up, **go to wmgbooks.com.**

About the Author
Dean Wesley Smith

Considered one of the most prolific writers working in modern fiction, *New York Times* and *USA Today* bestselling writer, Dean Wesley Smith published over two hundred novels and over seven hundred books in forty years, and hundreds and hundreds of short stories. He has over thirty million copies of his books in print.

At the moment he produces novels in four major series, including the time travel **Thunder Mountain** novels set in the old west, the galaxy-spanning **Seeders Universe** series, the cold case mystery series, **Cold Poker Gang** series, and the superhero series staring **Poker Boy.**

During his career, Dean also wrote a couple dozen *Star Trek* novels, the only two original *Men in Black* novels, Spider-Man and X-Men novels, plus novels set in gaming and television worlds. Writing with his wife Kristine Kathryn Rusch under the name Kathryn Wesley, they wrote the novel for the NBC miniseries **The Tenth Kingdom** and other books for *Hallmark Hall of Fame* movies.

He wrote novels under dozens of pen names in the worlds

of comic books and movies, including novelizations of almost a dozen films, from *X-Men* to *The Final Fantasy* to *Steel* to *Rundown*.

Dean also worked as a fiction editor off and on, starting at Pulphouse Publishing, then at *VB Tech Journal*, then Pocket Books, and now at WMG Publishing where he and Kristine Kathryn Rusch serve as executive editors for the acclaimed *Fiction River* anthology series. He took over the editorship of the acclaimed *Pulphouse Magazine* in 2018.

For more information about Dean's books and ongoing projects, please visit his website at www.deanwesleysmith.com

facebook.com/deanwsmith3

patreon.com/deanwesleysmith

bookbub.com/authors/dean-wesley-smith